M A D
addiction

JESSICA
SERRA HUIZENGA

books by

JESSICA SERRA HUIZENGA

Crazy Beautiful Series
Crazy Beautiful (Book 1)
Mad Addiction (Book 2)
(Look for Book 3 Coming Fall 2016!)

Author's Note:
While each story in the Crazy Beautiful Series can be read as a standalone book, I recommend reading them in order to fully understand the world and characters.

Kelley Brooks is saving herself for Prince Charming.
Ryan Blake, while charming, is definitely not a prince.

Always straightforward and realistic, Kelley Brooks and Ryan Blake know they are not right for each other. Kelley believes in fate and waiting for "the one" while Ryan prefers maintaining distance and control with unattached one-night stands.

But after indulging in a single, meaningless wedding hookup, unexpected circumstances force them into one hell of a complicated situation.

After agreeing to a fake engagement, both Ryan and Kelley must confront their pasts—and true feelings—causing them to question everything they thought they knew about family, commitment, and most importantly, love.

A lie brought them together, but will the truth tear them apart?
And what the heck does happily ever after really mean, anyway?

For the best mom I know, my own.

Your sacrifice, encouragement, and support have shaped who I am. When my world has felt either broken or whole, you have always been my one constant.

Love up. xx

CHAPTER

one

Kelley

"I CAN'T BELIEVE YOU, KINSLEY I-Don't-Need-Anyone-Else Moore, actually tied the knot. The same girl who, eight months ago, told me Prince Charming didn't exist. I don't know if I should laugh or cry."

Despite my teasing, I lean in to give my best friend a giant hug. She looks beautiful—simple white dress, brown hair set in loose curls, blue eyes dusted with a hint of sparkly shadow, and cheeks pink and glowing—but it's her sincere happiness that makes her truly radiant. She hugs me back and whispers so only I can hear, "Thanks for helping me believe in happy endings."

She pulls back and smiles such a genuine smile that I can't help but return it. In just a few short months I've witnessed first-hand how much Kinsley has changed, going from lonely and guarded and afraid of love to opening up, letting go, and committing to someone who is a perfect match for her in every way.

I swallow down an involuntary pang of jealousy. I really am happy for her.

I give Kinsley's hand a squeeze before setting my sights on her new husband. "And you, sir, better take care of her, or else." I pretend to threaten him with a stern glare, but from the way Lucas Graham looks at his bride, I know I don't have anything to worry about.

"Don't worry, Kell. You know I've got her back. Yours, too." Lucas winks before leaning down and enveloping me in his own friendly embrace. I've gotten to know him better over the last few months and know he can be trusted. Last night at the rehearsal dinner he even pulled me aside to thank me for not giving up on Kins five years ago when her parents were in a car accident and her jerk of an ex betrayed her and she had nobody else to look out for her. He doesn't have to thank me—I love Kins and will of course always be here for her—but I appreciate he took the time to acknowledge what our friendship means. After everything she's been through, Kinsley deserves someone as good and loyal as Lucas.

Now if only I could find my own perfect prince . . .

The night is winding down so I let Lucas and Kinsley get back to mingling and make my way between the crowded tables to the bar. While she doesn't have any family of her own, Kinsley insisted Lucas invite all of his to share in their special day. I imagine the whole idea of family means a lot more to her these days now that she actually has people she can trust in her life. I notice Eli, Lucas' father, leading Kinsley to the dance floor, and the look of adoration on both of their faces makes me tear up.

I never guessed my friend would have any sort of wedding, let alone such a traditional one. At first I questioned why she of all people would want to get married at a swanky place like Woodwind Hills, but since she admitted it's the spot Lucas and she first noticed each other, it makes perfect sense. Kinsley and I are pretty much polar opposites when it comes to believing in things like soul mates and fairy tale weddings . . . well at least we used to be. Now it's as if I'm staring at my own vision board come to life.

The thing is I can't help but feel somewhat envious of how this all ended up. Don't get me wrong, I am one hundred percent happy for Kinsley and Lucas, but I find it ironic that up until a few months ago Kinsley didn't even believe in love, yet here she is, marrying the man of her dreams.

I, on the other hand, have believed wholeheartedly in true love and saving myself for "the one" ever since my high school boyfriend-turned-fiancé and I broke up seven years ago. I thought we would be together for the long haul, but eventually realized it was a joke. Call me a hopeless romantic, but I still believe there is someone fate has in store for me, except never again will I try to change a guy—it's a waste of everyone's time. When I meet the right person to fall in love with I'll know, but until then I'll just have to wait. Which is why here *I* am, twenty-six years old, standing alone in a crowded room holding a now-empty glass of champagne.

Reality, you sure do suck sometimes.

I'm about to turn for a refill on my drink when I feel a presence right behind me. I smell the distinct, spicy sharpness of cinnamon, and I'd recognize it anywhere.

Ryan Blake, Lucas' best friend, reaches his muscular, tuxedo-clad arm in front of me with a flute of bubbly. "I think it's my duty, as best man of this fine affair, to keep the maid of honor company . . . and thoroughly hydrated." He places the full glass in my hand, reaching for the empty one and placing it on a high top table in front of us.

Ry and I first met close to a year ago when I, as her realtor, helped Kinsley rent a house from Eli. Ryan is his lawyer so we met at the lease signing, but we've had a few more clients in common since. Between occasional, brief work interactions and having mutual best friends, we've become familiar. I'll admit I only first noticed him for his looks—his tall, athletic frame with short, dark hair that always manages to look both messy and styled, and deep, blue eyes that are always cool and enticing—but I'm sorry to report he's not exactly soul mate material. It's a pretty well-known fact he's not the type to settle down. While I've never really heard him talk about his love life, I've certainly heard the rumors. The guy's middle name should be One-Night-Stand. He always looks so laid back and sure of himself it's no wonder women fall at his feet . . . or on his dick. Apparently he is quite skilled with that thing, so I've read on more than one bathroom wall. Couple that with the whole sexy, smart lawyer things he's got going on and there's no denying Ryan Blake is about as hot as they come.

But unfortunately his inability to commit means he's off limits for me. *Damn.*

"Gee, thanks." I take a drink of the champagne before nodding toward his own empty hands. "Aren't you going to join me?"

He just smirks and shakes his head. "Nah. I don't drink, so I'll have to watch you enjoy that enough for the both of us."

I tilt my head and try to tell if he's lying, but something about his self-assured demeanor makes me think he's not the type to make something up for the hell of it. "Really? Why's that?"

He looks out at the crowd, choosing his words carefully before turning back to me. "I used to drink. Too fucking much. So, now I don't." He puts his hands in his pockets and shrugs, as if it really is as simple as that.

We continue to stand in silence and people-watch around

the ballroom. A slow ballad starts playing, which means a bunch of couples—including the bride and groom—are snuggled out on the dance floor. I see Logan and Tristan, mutual friends of Lucas and Ryan, slow-grind with two girls who seem to be enjoying the open bar a little too much. Between the effects of the alcohol and my current mood, I must have quite the look on my face.

"So, planning any hot wedding hookups tonight?" Ryan smirks seductively.

I roll my eyes. Typical perverted man-talk. "I'm pretty sure harassing the maid of honor isn't part of your job description. Isn't there some slutty bimbo around to indulge your perverted fantasies?" I plaster on a fake, sweet smile. I was aiming for teasing rather than bitchy, but I'm already feeling frustrated without being reminded of my current love life . . . more accurately my lack thereof.

Ryan chuckles. "Ouch. Aw c'mon, Brooks. I'm just trying to make friendly conversation." He leans in to rest his arm on the table in front of us. "And I didn't mean me. There's a guy over there that can't seem to keep his eyes off you. Might be a good contender."

He nods toward an attractive blond haired man talking to an elderly couple across the room. The guy has a nice smile with straight, white teeth. Completing his all-American look are two adorable dimples dotting his cheeks. We make eye contact and he grins at me.

I take a moment to assess my reaction.

Nope, no butterflies. No spark. I break our gaze and shake my head. "Thanks, but I'll pass."

"Poor guy. You haven't even met him. What if he's the one and you don't even know it?" Ryan looks at me with a mocking tilt of his head. Last night at the rehearsal dinner he was around when Kinsley and I were talking and I may have mentioned something about waiting for the right guy when she pointed out some of Lucas' cousins. I bet he couldn't wait for the perfect opportunity to tease me about it.

"I just know. There's nothing there when I look at him. No . . . fireworks or anything."

Ryan opens and closes his mouth several times, but no words come out. I think I've rendered him speechless. He studies me intensely, trying to understand.

"What?" I try to explain. "I don't waste my time with random hookups when I know it won't lead to anything more."

He looks baffled before asking, "So you're telling me you refuse to have sex unless it comes with a fucking marriage proposal or something?" He chuckles, amused. "Don't tell me you're a virgin, too."

I'm not surprised by his unsympathetic questioning, but I am impressed with his unashamed bluntness. Most guys try to dance around the topic, but I find it much easier to lay it out up front.

"No." Not exactly. "I had a serious boyfriend in high school and college, and yes we had sex, so you can wipe that appalled look off your face. We broke up right before we graduated, and I realized I had already wasted too many years on him knowing it wouldn't last. I decided then that it would be pointless to screw around unless I knew there was a future with someone." I decide to leave out the part that we were engaged when I found out Jake was really just a lying sack of shit. I think back to a few months ago when I saw Ryan at a beach party and he basically admitted he has no plans to ever get serious. We may not agree on the end game, but we both can appreciate honesty. "As I've heard you, yourself, mention, there's no use in setting up any unrealistic expectations." He of all people should understand.

Ryan lets a devilish grin play across his lips. "Well this guy must have been a terrible fuck if he made you swear off sex for the past however many years. That's a damn shame." He gets more serious and stands up straight before formally stating, "On behalf of men everywhere, I personally want to apologize for such a misrepresentation of our general population's skills in the sack." He puts his hand to his chest, as if swearing a sincere oath, although a lighthearted chuckle breaks through.

I stiffen my shoulders, trying to exude confidence. This, after all, is *my* business, right? I can choose to do whatever I want. Or, in this case, *not* do.

Except when I finally hear myself say all of it out loud to someone as straightforward and unattached as Ryan Blake—and he calls me on it—it does seem kind of ridiculous.

"It's not because of that. I just. . . ." I trail off, unable to find the right words.

" . . . want fireworks?" Ryan cocks his eyebrow and looks softer as he finishes my thought.

I nod. "Yeah, something like that."

"Look," Ryan leans back down toward me. "In all seriousness, do you really think the world is going to end if you loosen up and have some fun? I mean I'm no expert, but going a few years without an orgasm has got to be against the laws of nature or something." The way he pretends to be genuinely concerned about my O status for the sake of my well-being makes me want to laugh.

Not wanting to let him get away with it, though, I lean in even closer. "Thanks for the concern, Blake, but let's just say I'm more than capable of keeping myself company." I give him a knowing look, and for a second I think he's surprised I'm willing to admit it.

He quickly recovers, getting so close I can feel his breath. He doesn't hide the way he moves his blue eyes down to my chest and lets them linger before returning them to lock onto mine. "Oh I have no doubt, Brooks. But you're telling me you don't sometimes want a little *company*?" The way he speaks in a deep, sexy voice and his eyes go glassy make me think he's picturing something extremely salacious. I can practically hear imaginary clothes ripping off from here.

And damn it if I don't feel a tingle between my legs.

Already feeling emotionally frustrated and confused, I try one last time to stand my ground, although I'm not sure who it's supposed to convince more . . . him or me.

I sigh. "What's the point? I believe there is someone out there for everyone . . . you know, like true love and all that? No use getting distracted in the meantime. My life has a plan, and I aim to stick to it."

Ryan leans back so we're not so close. He appears to be contemplating what I just said. "You really think that if you have sex—unattached, random, meaningless sex—tonight, that you might ultimately mess up your entire future with your supposed soul mate?"

I shrug, not sure what else to say. When he puts it like that it makes me question what I, myself, just argued. If we're saying the same thing, how come he makes it sound so much more irrational?

"Wow. You're mad, you know that, right?" Ryan laughs and shakes his head.

Regaining some clarity, along with a little defensive anger, I retaliate. "How about you tell me what's so great about random, meaningless sex, then. You'd rather have a string of one night stands than feel something real and serious?" I cross my arms, throwing in an accusatory glare.

Despite looking stung for a brief moment, without backing

down, Ryan continues. "Sex doesn't have to be meaningful for you to feel something. Hell, I feel all sorts of things when I'm with a girl, and I don't even have to know her name." He gets a smug, cocky look, but I catch a glimpse of something else in his eyes. Regret maybe? But it passes quickly and I'm reminded of what an arrogant ass he is.

Not wanting to let him off the hook, I scoff, "You sound like some sort of sex addict."

Ryan goes rigid and I see his jaw tick, but he remains calm and laid back when he speaks. "Addiction is a sign of weakness. It's selfish and reckless. I promise you, when it comes to women I am nothing if not straightforward and controlled. Sex can be anything you need it to be if you're honest and up front about it—hot, dirty, warm, loud, wild, and downright liberating. You can't knock it till you try it, sweetheart, so until you do I can't take what you say too seriously."

Then he winks.

I want that to disgust me, but it has the opposite effect. What the hell is wrong with me?

"So, what? You're telling me that I should go proposition Dimples over there,"—I motion to the man still chatting with the older couple—"for a quick romp in the bathroom before you'll admit what I have to say makes sense?"

Without missing a beat, Ryan retorts, "If you think that's what you need to do—and that he'll be the one to satisfy you— go ahead." He looks right at me with a smug coolness that is indifferent yet still somehow challenging. "But I think we both know there's a better chance of hell freezing over."

Now he's purposely trying to needle me.

And it's working.

"What's that supposed to mean?" I ask, now majorly insulted.

He throws his arms up in mock surrender. "Hey, you wouldn't want anything to derail your train to Prince Charming." He leans in closer before snidely adding, "I hear he's coming in on the 10 AM express tomorrow, so you don't want to chance missing him, right?"

He smiles in what I assume is meant to be a playful way, but it just gets my blood boiling. He keeps twisting my words around so they sound so pathetic.

OK, maybe it is a little pathetic to put my entire life on hold for some man I'm not sure exists yet. But I'll be damned if I let Ryan Blake think I'm helpless and naive. I might believe in things like true love and soul mates, but that doesn't have to mean I don't know how to live in the moment. It *has* been seven years . . . maybe it is time I have a little fun.

I down the rest of my glass of champagne in one gulp before pinning Ryan with an icy stare. "Good thing I'm both punctual *and* a morning person, then. But tonight, I think it's safe to say, is Mr. Wrong's lucky night." And with that I try to storm over to the man with the dimples.

Ryan grabs my arm to spin me back around toward his chest before I can get very far.

Oh, hello rock solid abs . . .

"Fuck, OK, hold on there, Brooks. I was just teasing you. There's no reason to go screw some random guy you've never met just to prove a point to me. I'm sorry." He looks genuinely apologetic as he squeezes my shoulder. The way he goes from cruel to kind in a matter of seconds confuses me.

I look into his eyes, wanting to make sure he knows I'm not some sort of clueless shrinking violet. "I'm not naive, Blake. I don't think that if I make one small, stupid decision now it will throw off my entire life. And even if it did, I make my own choices and deal with my own consequences."

Ryan's eyes get softer. "I respect that. I really do, Kell. It's your life, so it's your call how you choose to live it. But I can see you desperately need to let loose a little and I want to help. I just didn't think you'd be so feisty about it." He smiles and I feel a strange flutter in the pit of my stomach.

I cross my arms again, shielding both him from my *feistiness* and myself from his genuine stare. It'd be easier to hate him if he really was just a raging asshole, but the sad truth is he's simply able to put into words every doubt and fear I've always tried to ignore. I don't want to feel like I'm missing out on an experience because I'm too stubborn to admit I might be too idealistic.

And that makes me want to prove him—and myself—wrong even more.

"And how exactly do you plan to help?" I question flatly, trying to keep my curiosity from getting the best of me.

Ryan takes a moment to read me before leaning back against the table. "I have a proposition for you."

I raise my eyebrow, intrigued.

He continues, "One night—tonight. You and me. Unattached, random, meaningless sex. We both go in knowing exactly what it's meant to be—a brief fling to make each other feel good—and then tomorrow you can go back to waiting for Mr. Right and see that the world is still spinning like nothing ever happened."

I consider his proposal, trying not to linger on the fact that Ryan Blake just propositioned *me* to have sex. "And how is that any different from what I was going to do with Dimples?"

"Well for starters, I don't have a fucking sissy nickname like Dimples." He grunts, and I can't help but crack a small smile. "And secondly, you know I fully understand this arrangement going in. We know enough about each other that you can trust me, but we also don't know each other well enough for it to be awkward."

I don't agree, but I don't say no, either. Part of me is tired of waiting around for some faceless, nameless Mr. Right, and part of me (mainly the lower part) wants to know if all the rumors about Ryan are true. *Stupid horny hormones.*

I also realize I've gotten used to rationalizing my abstinence as waiting for "the one," but what if I'm really just scared? Ryan picks up on my hesitation. "Unless you still think this will somehow ruin you for your future husband . . ."

While he sounds sincere, the implied taunt gives me the courage to respond. I stand up straight, take a deep breath, and extend my hand. "Well, Blake, looks like you've got yourself a deal."

CHAPTER

two

Ryan

I SWEAR, GOING IN, I had no intention of seducing Kelley Brooks tonight.

But fuck me, that's sure as shit what I just did.

We shake on our deal and, without letting go of her hand, I lead her out of the room. I make my way toward the bathroom at the far end of the hall, knowing it's set out of the way and has a lock. Let's just say it's not the first time I've been down this particular path.

We may not agree on a lot of things, but something about the way Kelley is as straightforward as me is refreshing. It doesn't hurt she looks hot as hell, either. So why can't we have a little fun? It's only for tonight, which has been made perfectly clear.

My one non-negotiable rule about women is that they have to know the deal going in: sex is just sex, nothing more. There will be no cuddling. There will be no morning after phone calls.

And there sure as fuck will be no second dates.

And no, this doesn't mean I'm a heartless asshole, either. It just means I like to be up front. So yes, that might mean I come off as a dick, but at least I'm an honest dick. Which is why this deal with Kelley is perfect for both of us. We both know this isn't going anywhere, but who says we can't help each other out with a little temporary pleasure? Hell, better me than that douche with the dimples. Usually I wouldn't care what—or who—a woman does, but considering Kelley and I are sort of friends, the thought of some random asshole taking advantage of her makes me want to punch something. At least I know I'll be careful with her.

Given my history with addiction, I know to keep women at a distance. Sleeping together more than once leads to a pattern, a pattern leads to comfort, comfort leads to a relationship, and a relationship leads to dependence. I don't have the best track record when it comes to issues of dependency, so I choose to remove temptation. It's why I don't let girls into my apartment and why I keep my personal life just that. Fucking *personal*.

I glance back to make sure Kelley is keeping up in her tight dress and high heels. She looks confident, but nervous. I remember while this may not be new for me, it is for her. It's just sex, but I don't think a quickie against a bathroom sink is the best call on this one. Without breaking my stride, I turn left down the next hall and head for the door that leads outside. On the outskirts of the patio is a secluded storage house. I reach for the door, saying a silent *thank fucking god* that it's unlocked, and pull Kelley inside. It's cramped and dark, but beats being next to a toilet.

I close the door and latch it behind us, hesitating before making another move. She confirmed she's not a virgin, but, if she's only ever been with one guy and it's been years, there's still part of me that feels like an asshole. I just couldn't stand to see the frustration and defeat in her eyes when she talked about wait-ing for *"the one."* I barely know Kelley, but from the few times we've interacted I can tell she knows how to take care of herself, so why she lets a non-existent man dictate her sex life is beyond my fucking comprehension. She needs to loosen up and have a little harmless fun.

And I'm more than happy to be the one to help push her physical limits. If she wants me to, that is.

"What are you waiting for?" The patio lights outside provide just enough of a glow to make out Kelley's features. Her eyes look anxious, but her voice is calm.

I take a small step toward her. "Just want to make sure you're not having second thoughts." Another step. "Because once we get started, there's no going back."

She releases a breath. "Jesus, Blake. I may not typically screw guys at weddings like this, but that doesn't make me a fucking delicate flower." She closes the gap between us and reaches up to loosen my tie before adding, "I promise I'm not going to break, so you don't have to be gentle."

You don't have to tell me twice.

That's all the confirmation I need to crash my lips onto hers, and she reciprocates with just as much enthusiasm. Before I know it, my jacket and shirt are being cast off, fast and frantic.

I reach behind her to unzip the dark purple dress that fits her like a glove, pushing it down her round shoulders, past the dip of her small waist, over the curve of her full hips, and down her long, toned legs. Soon she is standing before me in nothing but a pair of heels and a strapless bra, complete with matching panties. Her long brown hair is twisted up behind her head. A few loose pieces hang down the sides of her face. She pauses, letting me admire her. I let my gaze scan her body before settling on her eyes. One is blue and one is brown and they manage to say so much about her that it's damn hard to look away. She stares at me with equal parts innocent lamb and devilish sex-kitten which drives me insane. I grab her and pull her to the floor over me. What better way to let her feel empowered than have her on top where she has full control?

Our tongues continue exploring each other's mouths as I help her get the rest of my clothes off. I can taste the slightest hint of champagne on her sweet lips, and that alone is intoxicating enough to make me want more. She moves expertly over me and I wonder if the near-virgin thing was all an act. For a girl who doesn't do this kind of thing, she sure as shit got the hang of it quickly. It's as if I've rubbed a magic lamp that unleashed a majorly hot sex genie.

And I'm just the lucky fucking bastard who's about to have all of his wishes come true . . .

I reach for my wallet to pull out a condom and move swiftly to get it on as she starts to grind her hips against mine. I push her underwear aside and swipe my fingers across her slit, making sure she's wet and ready, before she slowly—but deliberately—slides herself onto me.

I lie still in order to give her time to adjust, but once I'm fully buried inside her she only needs to take one deep breath before rocking her hips back and forth, increasing the speed and rhythm of our bodies.

Her hands grip my shoulders tightly and I hold her steady at her waist. I push my hips to slam up into her. She closes her eyes and bites her lip. For a split second I think I might be hurting her, but then she tosses her head back and a soft—definitely pleasurable—moan escapes from the base of her throat. She moves her hips at a perfect pace, allowing me to meet each of her thrusts.

She rides me for what seems like both forever and not long enough before I feel her muscles clench and convulse as she falls apart with her hands against my chest, crying out in pleasure, which is surprisingly all it takes for me to join her a second later.

We lay still, the sound of our labored breathing the only noise in the air. I'm still trying to recover when Kelley gracefully pushes herself off me and begins to re-adjust her clothes. I sit up on my elbows, damp with sweat and unable to fully comprehend what the fuck just happened while Kelley shimmies back into her dress.

As she zips herself up she glances over at me and coolly says "Guess you were right, Blake. Sex can be fun *and* meaningless. So, thanks for that."

In my head I know this means nothing, but for some reason the way she's so easily able to grasp this casual thing like a seasoned pro makes me feel fucking weird. Something about the way she pressed her hands against my heart as she came felt . . . intimate. Or maybe her talk about true love and soul mates and all that crap got stuck in my head. Or maybe I feel guilty for being the one to pop her random-hookup cherry. I shake it off. Clearly she's able to handle it like a champ, so no harm done, right?

Thankfully the blood has a chance to start flowing throughout the rest of my body again, and I'm able to respond with a cocky, "My pleasure."

I hoist myself off the floor to clean up with the handkerchief from my jacket pocket and pull my own clothes back on. Not caring for the awkward silence, I break it by pretending to examine the ceiling before stating, "Huh. And look at that . . . the sky hasn't fallen or anything." She scoffs as I plaster on a big grin and reach for the door, nodding toward the main building. "Now come on, Brooks. Let's get you back out there so you can meet Mr. Right."

CHAPTER

three

Four Weeks Later

Kelley

TWO PINK LINES.

That's all it takes to indicate how royally screwed I am.

Two. Pink. Fucking. Lines.

This is what I get for messing with fate and riding Ryan Blake in a storage shed like some sort of sex fiend.

It's all his fault.

OK, *half* his fault.

Truth is I have no one to be mad at but myself. As much as he might have been involved, Ryan never forced me to do anything. If memory serves, I was more than willing to be an eager participant. Now that I know that kind of intense bliss, I do kinda wonder how I've gone without it all these years. I'll never admit it out loud, but maybe Ryan was right; maybe my ex really was just bad at sex. Even though it meant nothing, I felt more connected to Ryan than I ever did with Jake.

As I sit here staring at the positive pregnancy test, I'm hit with a flood of emotions . . . emotions I've refused to think about for the past seven years . . .

Seven Years Ago

"HEY, BABE. I JUST GOT off the phone with my mom. She wants you to call her to talk about some wedding shit. I still don't understand why you two are planning this so soon. I told you both this will be a long engagement. I want to graduate and get a job and start to establish myself."

Jake comes through the front door to my tiny, shared apartment and throws his coat on the counter. He immediately walks to the fridge to grab a beer and I'm too excited to notice he barely looks at me, let alone kisses me hello. He turns around and takes a swig of his beer, finally noticing I'm standing there, hands behind my back, about ready to burst.

He looks annoyed as he shrugs at me. "What?"

I smile even bigger as I move my arms in front of me, revealing the small plastic stick.

Jake stares at it, looking confused. "What the fuck is that?"

I hold it out and can't help but giggle in delight. "We're going to have a baby, babe!"

I wait for him to understand and match my enthusiasm, but he just hangs his head and looks both tired and pissed.

"Jake?"

He lets out a big breath before yelling, "Damn it, Kelley. I can't deal with this shit right now. Don't you think we have enough going on without a baby ruining it?"

I physically retract at his harsh tone. He notices and slowly comes over to me, patting my shoulders and softening his tone. "Come on, babe. You have to admit this is bad timing. Don't you think we should wait?"

I try to hold back tears that threaten to fall. "I didn't plan for this, Jake. But it's happened and it's too late, now."

He pulls me closer to him and rubs his hands down my back. "It's not too late, Kell. I know this clinic and they—"

I snap my eyes up to his, pushing him back. "Are you seriously saying what I think you're saying?"

He looks at my pleadingly. "I'm sorry. I know, it's stupid. Forget I mentioned it. I'm only thinking of us . . . of our future. Please don't look at me like that. We're about to graduate and start our lives. Don't you understand?"

His voice is quiet and sincere, and I don't want to argue. All we seem to do lately is fight, and I'm afraid I'll lose him. Maybe he's right. I swallow down my previous excitement and feel numb as I nod and let him hug me. He whispers that we'll figure it out and I give in and let my tears fall, feeling empty and sad.

Over the next week, Jake seemed to be more excited about the baby, but I could feel the resentment he carried toward me. I tried my best to make it work, even though I knew in my heart we had grown apart a long time ago. I tried to convince myself a baby would bring us closer, but when I woke up to find my sheets soaked in red a week later, I knew it was fate's way of telling me our relationship was completely, painfully, and undoubtedly over.

My memories of Jake fade as I choose instead to recall the way Ryan felt moving under and inside me . . . how his mouth tasted like cinnamon . . . how his hands left my skin feeling hot . . .

My lady parts involuntarily contract, seeming to argue it was more than worth it. But then my brain kicks in with the rational realization that I am once again carrying the child of a man who is most definitely *not* Mr. Right, and I feel like I'm going to hurl. Whether it's morning sickness or just a harsh dose of reality, either way it blows.

This is *so* not a part of my life plan.

When my period was late I thought it was just my hormones being thrown out of whack since it has been a while (OK, let's be honest, it was the first time ever) that I felt that much pleasure, but lately I can barely keep my eyes open, I'm eating my weight in peanut M&Ms, I pee about five thousand times a day, and it feels like someone sucker-punched my boobs.

So here I am: pregnant, alone, and hiding in the office bathroom.

Earlier I convinced myself there was no way I was actually pregnant—I mean he used a condom for crap sake. But since I couldn't focus on anything else, I grabbed a test during lunch thinking it would come back negative and I could get on with my life. After the first one was positive I hoped it was a mistake, but after six glasses of water and five tests later, I think it's finally starting to sink in.

If I'm being honest, though, deep down I knew, even from the first positive reading. There's always a risk when we make certain choices. Especially when we know those choices aren't necessarily 100% effective. I'm not stupid enough to wonder how this happened. Oh, I know how it happened all right . . . I just didn't want to believe it could happen to *me*. I'm one of *those* girls now. The 2%. A statistic.

For a split second I let my mind wander to consider my options, but as quickly as the painful thought enters my mind, I know in my heart it's not an option. It never has been. I look down at the two little pink lines, and suddenly they don't seem that bad. Scary as hell? Definitely. But I'll find a way to handle it. I made my bed on the floor of that dark and dirty storage shed, and now I intend to lie in it.

Alone this time. Alone and fully clothed.

The creak of the bathroom door opening yanks me from my thoughts.

I recognize our receptionist's soft voice. "Kelley, are you in here?"

I quickly stash the plastic stick I'm still holding into my purse with the others. "Yeah, I'll be out in a sec."

"OK, I'll tell Mr. Burton. The broker for that building across town is here to go over terms of the potential contracts so he's looking for you."

Shit. I forgot we had that meeting this afternoon. I stand in the small stall and take a deep breath before grabbing my bag and unlatching the door. I breeze over to the sink and wash my hands. "I just have to grab my files from my desk. I'll be right there."

I smile a calm, collected smile as Gemma nods and scurries back out into the hall.

I wipe my hands on the hand towel before catching my own reflection in the mirror. Almost automatically, I lift my arm to brush a hand across my stomach.

Well, kid, I hope you're comfortable in there, 'cause there is no way I'm letting you go. We're kind of stuck with each other.

AFTER DROPPING MY BAG IN my office and grabbing my folder labeled *Grind* I head toward the conference room down the hall. Our client, Caleb Jones, is hoping to open a coffee house across town, but the men in charge of leasing the spot he wants are being difficult. They say they have a lot of offers on the place, but we convinced them to come and hear us out. My boss, Scott Burton, is already seated across from another man as I glide into the seat next to him, trying not to draw too much attention to the fact I'm late. Or growing a tiny human.

Thankfully they're still making small talk so I have a minute to organize my papers and thoughts. I've done a lot of work to help Caleb, and I refuse to let my recent revelation distract me from my job. Up until recently I've focused mainly on our residential accounts, so I'm grateful Mr. Burton has been letting me learn about the commercial side of things. As both a real estate broker and an attorney, he already has more work than he can handle, and, since I passed my own broker's license exam to become an associate six months ago, he's been giving me a lot more responsibility in general. I can only imagine how thrilled he'll be when he finds out about my current *situation*. As if I didn't already have enough to worry about . . .

"Mr. Andrews, we can't thank you enough for agreeing to sit with us today. This is my associate, Kelley Brooks." My boss gestures toward me and the stodgy looking man across the conference table nods at the introduction.

Just as I get ready to launch into my spiel about why *Grind* would be such a great addition to the area, the opening of the conference room door catches everyone's attention. When I see who walks through, I nearly hurl again.

Ryan fuck-me-on-the-floor Blake.

"Sorry I'm late. Traffic was a nightmare." He reaches out to shake Scott's hand. "Mr. Burton." And then he gets a cocky, damn delicious grin on his face as he nods my way. "Ms. Brooks. Good to see you again."

I stare blankly in response while he sits next to Mr. Andrews, adjusting his tie as he settles in. Mr. Andrews explains, "I hope you don't mind, but I asked Ryan here to consult on this with me. He's familiar with the legal aspects of our client's real estate dealings so I thought he could be a valuable asset."

My boss follows up with, "No problem at all. We're just getting started. Actually, Ryan, Kelley was just about to go over some of the details."

Ryan eyes me with an intrigued expression. "Great. Can't wait to hear it."

Suddenly I can't remember anything I was about to say. I'm not ready to deal with this thing inside me, *and* him all at the same time, but he's a friggin' walking, talking reminder. I didn't know he had anything to do with this meeting, and to say I'm caught off guard is the understatement of the year. It's like I think he will somehow know I'm pregnant just by looking at me, but the way he—and everyone else—stares at me obliviously, I realize I have to get it together.

I clear my throat and force myself to focus on the notes in front of me. "Well, as noted in Mr. Jones' letter of intent, we think *Grind* will offer something new for this location. It's not another cold, corporate coffee chain, but a neighborhood place with a deep respect for quality. And while independent coffee shops equal twelve billion dollars in annual sales, it's more than just numbers. Caleb is committed to offering a one-of-a-kind experience that we think people will really respond to. Rather than an impersonal place, *Grind* will be a local institution that will benefit the entire town."

I smile confidently, making sure to keep my focus on Mr. Andrews rather than the distracting man next to him.

Mr. Andrews looks impressed, and just when I think I've got him on the hook, Ryan interjects. "If I may, we have no doubt that Mr. Jones here is proposing a promising idea, but our client does want to make sure that he can get someone to commit for the long haul. He's asking for at least a five-year lease, which is a big commitment for any new business. We just want to make sure *Grind* is sustainable and won't be some passing fad."

He leans back and shrugs with an adorable tilt of his head. The man is good.

Oh my god, he's a lawyer. *A good one. Think he'll try to fight me for custody?*

Good god, my hormones are already out of control. What the hell? Focus, Kell. He doesn't even know about the kid yet—probably won't want anything to do with it anyway—and he basically just tried to shut you down on this deal. *Smug bastard.*

I sit up straighter. "Considering fifty percent of Americans drink an average of two to three cups of coffee per day, suffice it to say I don't think this is just a fad. Unless you think one hundred and fifty million people are suddenly going to decide to stop caffeinating, I think Caleb is a pretty safe bet. He already has a lot of local support, and, as we noted in the letter, he is more than willing to commit to a five-year lease given there's no escalation clause."

I cross my arms casually and give him my own superior look.

Maybe I won't even tell him I'm pregnant. Should I tell him? I guess he maybe sort of has a right to know, even if I don't expect anything from him . . .

He just smiles, unaffected. "Very true, Ms. Moore. Looks like someone certainly knows how to fight for her client. It's good to know you believe so strongly in him." His blue eyes stay trained on me, bright and amused.

Will the baby have his eyes?

Damn it all to hell. How am I ever going to survive the next nine months if I can't even get through one stupid meeting? I haven't had time to process what's happening in the first place, let alone what role Ryan will play in it . . . anatomically or otherwise.

Thankfully Mr. Andrews breaks the silence by tapping his fingers on the table, flipping through the packet we put together which includes the *Grind* business plan. "We certainly have a lot of great information to bring back to our client. He's sorry he couldn't make it today, but business has him traveling. Ryan and I will discuss it with him, though, and let you know as soon as he makes a decision."

Mr. Burton gets up to shake hands with Mr. Andrews and Ryan, and I politely stand and nod my goodbyes in their direction, using the large conference table as a buffer. I'm afraid if I'm in close proximity to Ryan I'll be intoxicated by his usual delicious scent, and I need a clear head right now. I noticed him subtly chewing a piece of gum when he spoke earlier. I bet that's why he always smells—and tastes—like cinnamon.

Once the two men leave the room I mumble some sort of grateful response to my boss' encouragements, then head back to my office as fast as I possibly can.

I round the corner to my doorway and am almost knocked flat on my ass as I come face to face with Ryan.

Startled, I blurt out, "What are you doing here?"

He hooks his thumb to the side, pointing toward the direction we just came from. "Didn't we go over this? I'm consulting for Mr. Andrews."

I walk to stand on the other side of my desk, needing to put as much distance between us as possible. "I know *that*, but what are you doing here, in my office?"

He casually puts his hands in his pockets and shrugs. "I wanted to say hi."

I stare at him, feeling suspicious and confused. "Hi."

He grins back. "Hey."

The way he looks at me in such an easygoing, unaware way weakens my defenses. Poor guy has no idea my uterus is growing something with half his DNA right this very minute as we stand here making small talk. At first I feel sorry for him, but that's quickly replaced by a wave of sickness. I need to sit down.

I plop myself down, resting my elbows on the desk and my chin in my hands as Ryan sits back comfortably in one of the armchairs sitting across from my desk. "So, how've you been?"

Before I can take a minute to compose an appropriate thought, I hear myself blurt out, "Pregnant, and you?"

Way to rip the Band-Aid off, Kell.

The look on Ryan's face is priceless. If I weren't too busy silently freaking myself out, I'd take a picture.

He barely blinks as he stares at me, almost *through* me, and his relaxed smile morphs to a confused scowl before his entire face goes blank. His Adam's apple bobs slowly. I'm pretty sure he swallows his gum.

He sits completely still for a good thirty seconds. I furrow my brow as I grow legitimately concerned.

Emotion finally returns to his features as his eyes focus back on me, although he still looks pale. "I'm sorry, what?"

I let out a deep breath before gesturing first at my stomach, then between us. "Pregnant. You know . . . me . . . you . . . storage shed . . ." I glance off to the side, avoiding eye contact as I trail off. I can feel my cheeks turn pink and a flush spread across my face as I recall our reckless romp.

Ryan pinches his eyes shut before taking his own deep breath. "But we . . . are you sure?"

Without saying anything, I remain remarkably calm as I push myself up from my chair and walk over to the office door. I shut it before sauntering back over to my desk where I pull out my purse. I unzip the gold zipper and unceremoniously dump the hoard of plastic sticks onto the smooth wood before sinking back into my chair.

Again, Ryan's face is priceless.

He stares at the pile of pregnancy tests. He lifts his arm as if he might reach out for one, but then drops it back down and looks uncomfortably around the room. He gets up, rubbing the back of his neck before looking back at me. "Are you sure it's mine?"

"Unless this thing has been cooking for seven years, then yes, I'm sure it's yours." I answer dryly. I hate to say it, but I am in no way surprised by his reaction. I am, however, a bit offended since I'm pretty sure we exhausted the fact I'm not the type to sleep around. Does he think I turned into some kind of nympho after our night together?

He looks at me apologetically before glancing subtly to the side, avoiding my eyes. "Are you going to keep it?" he asks in a soft yet honest voice.

I slink down in my chair a little further, leaning my head back against the soft leather. I subconsciously choose to rest my arms protectively across my stomach, fingers linked. I know this situation is completely different than what happened with Jake, so I try my best not to take out my anger and hurt on Ryan, no matter how much I feel the familiar sting. I knew going in that we would never have any type of relationship, and this baby isn't going to change that.

"Yes. But I want you to know I don't expect anything from you. I just thought you had a right to know."

Ryan starts to pace, although the small room doesn't allow for much maneuvering. As soon as he reaches one wall he only has to take about two steps to turn around and reach the other. *Step. Step. Turn. Step. Step. Turn.* Without stopping, he pulls a packet of gum out of his pocket and pops two pieces in his mouth, chewing rapidly.

"How long have you known?"

I glance at the clock. "About an hour."

"When are you due?" *Step, step, turn.*

"Not sure yet."

He picks up his pace, which makes me dizzy. "Have you been to the doctor?" Before I even have a chance to respond, "Does anyone else know? Do you eat salmon? I heard somewhere pregnant women should eat salmon or some shit. Fuck, where do you buy diapers?" *Step-step-turn-step-step-turn-step-step-turn.*

He continues to mumble incoherent ramblings about vitamins and Volvos. I almost find his panic adorable, but the more he goes on the more I can tell he really is losing his shit, something that clearly doesn't happen often. Maybe it's my maternal instinct kicking in, but I have to resist the urge to hold him close and run my hands down his back until he calms down. I interrupt him instead by stretching my hands on top of the desk. "Blake, can you please stop pacing, it's making me nauseous." He stops dead in his tracks, but I can tell his mind is still racing. "Look, I don't know what the hell to do either, but freaking out isn't going to do either of us any good. Chill for a second. I mean it when I say I don't expect anything from you. There's no reason this should mess up both of our lives."

He seems to take my advice about calming down since he leans forward to grip the back of the armchair, closes his eyes, and takes a deep breath. When he reopens them a moment later he's back to calm, cool, and collected Ryan.

"You're right, I'm sorry." He pushes himself off the chair and puts his hands in his pockets. "I just wasn't expecting this."

I sigh. "You and me both."

He softens his eyes before asking, "How do you feel?" His words, while sincere, sound raw, like he himself is surprised to have asked such a personal question. Yes, we've talked in depth about our sex lives, but somehow this seems more intimate. The way he looks at me with such intensity makes me believe he's genuinely interested to know the truth—and that he's asking about more than my physical state—but then again he's probably just being polite. I am, after all, carrying his spawn.

"I'm fine. I mean, I'm not *fine*, but I will be. This wasn't exactly part of the plan, but I'll figure it out."

"And you really think you're going to do it on your own?"

Something about the tone of his voice makes me feel defensive. "Of course, why wouldn't I? Neither of us planned for this to happen, and I've known from the beginning what kind of guy you are. I'm not going to try and trap you or anything." I act as nonchalant as possible, really hoping the fact that I'm actually scared shitless doesn't show through.

He cocks his eyebrow and pins me with an unforgiving stare. "And exactly what kind of guy am I? The asshole kind that will abandon his own fucking kid?"

Crap. In my attempt to let him off the hook I've obviously made him angry.

"Come on Blake, I don't see it like that. But I know you aren't interested in any sort of commitment, and even if you were, we both know we're not right for each other. We had one night. That's all it was supposed to be. That's all it was." *Wasn't it?*

I see his jaw tense and it looks like he's trying real hard not to lose it. When he speaks, his voice is level and measured. "I'm not going to walk away, Kelley. This is for both of us to deal with, not just you."

His forceful determination should feel threatening, but honestly I find it comforting. I also know it won't change anything. Even if he is going to stick around for the baby, it's certainly not to be with me, and I don't know how to make that work. It's one thing to accept I'll be a single mother who got knocked up after a one-night stand. It's another to believe we're some kind of family.

I slump back in my chair, exhausted from trying to deal with all of this at once. "Let's not make any decisions now. I mean I haven't even been to the doctor yet. I'll make an appointment and we'll see what happens after that, OK? There's nothing we can do this second anyway so let's both just get back to work."

Ryan must be just as emotionally spent, because he agrees without any further argument, although he makes me promise to let him know when the appointment is so he can clear his calendar. I'm too drained to protest.

Before he leaves he asks one more time how I'm feeling, and I again assure him I'm fine.

I'm about to have a child with a guy who is not only NOT the one, but not even my husband or boyfriend. Hell, he's barely even a friend. I'm friggin' fan-fucking-tastic.

CHAPTER

four

Five Weeks

Ryan

"DUDE, YOU LOOK LIKE YOU haven't slept in days. If I didn't know better I'd say you must be in love or some shit."

"Fuck off."

Except Lucas is right. About the sleeping part, that is. I've barely slept for the past week. Every time I shut my damn eyes all I can see is the fear in Kelley's. If anyone happened to be listening in on our conversation last week, it might have sounded like she had her shit together about everything, but I could tell she's terrified and unsure. I would never leave her to deal with this alone, but fuck if I'm not just as unsure about being a dad. How in the hell am I going to do this?

It's bad enough I'm the only person she let into her pants in seven fucking years, but then the goddamned condom had to go and break. Fuck, I'm never having sex again.

Whoa, OK, let's not be rash. Next time at least make sure the girl is on the pill, just in case.

Except I have a feeling next time definitely won't be any time soon. They call that shit birth control for a reason, and right now I don't feel anything like I have this fucking birth stuff under control.

I'm sitting on my giant leather couch with my head resting on the back, my arms and legs slack as I stare at the ceiling. Lucas is in the matching recliner across from me, looking straight up amused. I guess I deserve it for all the crap I usually give him.

"And cranky, too. Either it's that time of the month or something else is going on." He leans back, linking his hands behind the back of his head. "I assume it's the reason you begged me to leave my beautiful wife home alone to babysit your sorry ass."

"I never beg, asshole." I love the guy like a brother, but he knows he can give me shit. It's how we communicate. We give each other a hard time, but at the end of the day we always have the other's back.

I've been so caught up in my own goddamn head about everything I thought I could use someone to talk to. Am I ready to hear it all out loud again? I know if I'm going to tell someone, though, Luc is the only person I trust.

Will he give me crap about it? Damn straight. But at least he won't judge.

Luc lets me sit in silence for a few minutes longer, understanding I'll talk when I'm ready.

Without lifting my head, I squeeze my eyes shut and pinch the bridge of my nose with my right hand. I hate drawing shit out, so let's get this over with. "Man, I screwed up. I fucked Kelley Brooks at your wedding and now she's fucking pregnant."

After a moment of silence all I hear is Luc mutter his own, *"Fuck."*

I drop my hand and let out a deep breath. "Yeah."

I hear Lucas shift forward in the recliner. "That's what this is about."

Lucas nods to the unopened bottle of Jack Daniels sitting on the coffee table between us. He must have seen it as soon as he came in, but he knows me well enough to guess it wouldn't be sitting here without a significant reason.

I swallow thickly, but don't respond. I don't have to.

Luc changes the subject. "What happens now? Are you two, like, *together*?"

I lift my head. "No." I don't know what the hell we are. "But I respect her and nobody else knows anything yet so this is between us. I don't think she's even told Kinsley, so not a word."

"How does Kelley feel about it?"

"She says she's fine and she'll figure out how to deal with it on her own, but I'm sure as hell not going to walk away. I may not know the first thing about parenting, but I learned one or two things *not* to do, and ignoring your kid is pretty high at the top of that list." I plop my head back down. "Even though I'll still probably fuck it up. Kelley's life, and the kid's."

Luc contemplates a thought. "Just because your parents were shitty doesn't mean you will be, too. We already know you don't subscribe to their particular brand of bullshit."

My mother, Holly Blake, is your quintessential rich, superficial snob, caring only about appearances and perceptions. Growing up, as long as people thought we were the perfect family, that was all that mattered. If she refused to acknowledge a problem, then it simply didn't exist. And believe me, my sister and I were nothing but problems. When my dad walked out when we were kids, leaving my mom to deal with us on her own, she pretended everything was fine. He didn't want to deal with us, and she chose to ignore everything, which is exactly why I try to be honest and straightforward now. It might be harsh, but it beats being fake or afraid like them. With a lot of self-determination I managed to turn my life around, but our relationship has always been fucked up. I'm civil with my mom for my sister Hazel's sake, but I mainly keep to myself.

"That doesn't necessarily mean I'm immune from the Blake DNA either. Commitment isn't our strong suit . . . unless it's something self-destructive, that is."

Lucas leans forward, resting his elbows on his knees. "You've been sober for ten years, Ry. That's a pretty big fucking commitment if you ask me. What makes you think you won't have the same determination when it comes to your own kid?"

"Yeah, and it only took about two days after finding out I'm going to be a father before I went out and bought this fucking thing." I motion toward the bottle of Jack, feeling frustrated. Mainly at myself for being so weak.

Lucas pushes himself to his feet and grabs the bottle off the table. He holds it in his hand and stares at it intently. He shifts his eyes to me and shrugs matter-of-factly. "But you didn't drink it."

He casually tosses the bottle in my lap and heads to the door.

Right before he lets himself out, he adds, "I know you'll do the right thing."

I'm left alone to stare at the bottle.

Fuck, I just wish I knew what that is.

I think back to my tenth birthday, the last time I saw my father.

My mom threw this huge party—complete with magicians, face painters, and a waterslide—which, looking back, should have been the first sign something was wrong. She always overcompensates with some fake ass "Look How Popular and Rich I

Am" party when she knows damn well her life is superficial and empty. I remember thinking I was the coolest little shit that day, oblivious to anything going on around me.

After we had cake and opened presents I wanted to show my dad the remote control car I got and went inside to find him. When I got to my parent's bedroom door I overheard them talking. My mom said something about by him leaving her alone to deal with his kids and he responded that he didn't care and we weren't his problem anymore. He said he couldn't stand her and their life together was a mistake and he was going to move on without us.

As he left the room, suitcase in hand, smelling like the same bottle of bourbon he always drank, he passed me without saying a word. I called for him from the top of the stairs just as he reached the front door, but he never looked back. My mom came out of the room a minute later, also walked right past me, and went downstairs to talk to some of the guests like nothing ever happened. From that point on any time my sister or I tried to mention him, she would mumble something about a business trip and change the subject. Eventually we stopped asking.

Years later I realized what a selfish bastard my father was and knew I would never choose to have a family if it meant I was going to be anything like him. I still can't comprehend how he could just leave. My mom may have her own problems, but no woman deserves to be treated like that. I might not picture a future with any of the girls I fuck, but I make sure they know that so there are no mistakes and no regrets.

And now that I'm faced with this impossible situation with Kelley, I'm scared to fucking death I'll turn out just like dear old dad anyway.

Fuck. My. Life.

CHAPTER

five

Six Weeks

Kelley

"I'M SORRY, COULD YOU REPEAT that? I thought you just said you're pregnant with Ryan Blake's baby, but I must seriously need my hearing checked."

Kinsley stares at me, looking doubtful. I nod, trying to hold back tears. Damn, these hormones need to chill.

Kinsley's eyes soften as she looks wistfully at my stomach. "Well, I guess that explains why you look different. You're glowing."

She smiles but I can't help but answer dryly, "I'm bloated."

She leans forward and pats my stomach playfully. "Aww, you're already growing a bump!"

I swat her hand away. "No, it's just a blump." I slink down

in one of her kitchen chairs. "It's only been a few weeks and I already feel like a bloated cow."

"What did the doctor say?"

"Beats me. My first appointment is in two weeks."

Kinsley sits in her own chair across from me, looking eager as she rests her chin in her hands.

I mimic her pose, looking a little less thrilled. "Ugh, what am I going to do, Kins?"

"Live happily ever after?" She raises an eyebrow and smirks playfully.

I roll my eyes. "Yeah, except for one minor detail."

"What's that?"

"Um, the fact that Ryan is not exactly Prince Charming?" I lean back, crossing my arms over my chest.

Kinsley questions, "Are you sure about that? Seems to me like it might be fate . . ."

The word fate makes my stomach roll. "No, this is fate's way of telling me to go screw myself. In fact, if I had stuck to that I wouldn't be in this mess to begin with."

Kinsley smiles suggestively. "I dunno, Kell. I always thought there was something between you two."

I eye her, unamused. "I liked you better when you were cynical."

Kinsley laughs before getting up to put water in the teakettle. Once she fills it and adjusts the knob on the stovetop, she turns back to face me. "In all seriousness, did you talk to Ryan? What did he say?"

"I told him I didn't expect anything from him, but he said he wants to help. I'm just not sure what that means. We had an agreement that it was only going to be one night together. I don't think we should let it go beyond that."

Kinsley rests her hands on the counter behind her. "I don't

think you really have a choice at this point. Like it or not you'll always be connected to him now. I mean it's not like you can expect to never see him again."

I know Kinsley is right, but I like pretending this can be simple. The fact remains Ryan Blake is not some complete stranger I can ignore. When word gets out he's the father, I don't know that I can take people thinking I am just another notch in his belt . . . one that was stupid enough to get herself knocked up by a man who told her the deal up front. One night, and one night only. Meaningless sex and nothing more. God, I'll seem like a complete idiot. I can kiss Mr. Right goodbye forever . . . nobody will want me now.

"Look, I don't know what I'm going to do about it, but promise me you won't say anything? I mean it, Kins, you can't even tell Luc. I need to figure out what I'm going to do, first."

Kinsley pours some of the now boiling water into a mug and sets it in front of me. "I promise, but sooner or later it's going to have to come out."

I twist the paper at the end of the tea bag in my fingers. I know she's talking about the secret and the not the actual baby, but I respond with, "I know, but hopefully in nine months I'll have a better plan."

Eight Weeks

RYAN AND I PULL UP to the Women's Health Center at 9:50 am. My appointment is at 10, and Ryan showed up at my doorstep at 9:30. Our conversation went a little something like this:

Me: irked "I thought I told you to meet me at the clinic?"
Ryan: shrugs "I decided to drive you."
Me: hands on my hips "You know I'm perfectly capable of doing

this myself."

Ryan: *cocky, amused smirk* "I know."

And then he held open the passenger door to his truck as if there was no point arguing. Polite jerk.

I'm confused enough about our relationship . . . or lack of one . . . without him pretending to care. It doesn't help I am feeling extra anxious today, which translates to me being extra bitchy. Ryan and I haven't seen each other much the past couple weeks, even though he checks on me via text. When he asks how I'm feeling I want to scream at the phone "What do you care?!" but I actually find it incredibly sweet, so I end up feeling even more confused than ever.

Once inside I give my name to the receptionist and she hands me a clipboard of paperwork to fill out. Ryan and I both glance around the waiting room at the three other women already seated: A blond who looks like she's barely eighteen with a stomach as round as a beach ball, a middle-aged brunette looking frazzled with a toddler at her feet and a hand on her swollen stomach, and a dark-haired girl nursing a newborn. I make my way over to one of the empty chairs, but Ryan hangs back, chewing nervously on a piece of gum. He looks uncomfortable as he leans against the wall next to me.

"Aren't you going to sit down?" I motion toward the empty seat next to me.

The newborn starts to cry, and Ryan looks like he's about ready to pass out. "Nah, I'm good."

I shrug and begin filling in the forms. "Suit yourself."

I scribble the pen across the paper when Ryan suddenly blurts out, "Your middle name is Sunshine?" He lets out a loud chuckle as he looks over my shoulder.

I move to hold the clipboard to my chest, shielding the rest of the information from his view. "Shut up."

He grins and looks like he wants to say something else, but doesn't.

I stare up at him. "What?"

"Nothing. I like it."

A nurse opens the door across from us. "Ms. Brooks? We're ready for you."

Ryan pushes himself off the wall and nods toward the doorway as he tries to contain a smile. "Come on, Sunshine." He still looks adorably amused, and the fact I think he's cute makes me want to throw up.

I choose instead to roll my eyes and slam the clipboard into his chest as I breeze past.

The nurse looks at Ryan and then to me before hesitantly asking, "Would you like your . . . husband to join?"

I look at Ryan who just gives me a shit-eating grin. The hot bastard is enjoying this.

I smile sweetly at the nurse. "Sure. But he's not my husband. He's just the sperm donor." The nurse looks uncomfortable and confused. Ryan flashes her a charming smile as she leads us into exam room three.

The nurse grabs a paper gown and places it on the exam table. "You can remove your pants and underwear and drape this over your lap." I stare at the gown. I thought they'd only need to see my stomach? As if sensing my hesitancy, she explains, "A transvaginal ultrasound gives us a clearer picture this early on." She lets us know the doctor will be in soon and closes the door behind her as she leaves.

I grab the gown and stare at Ryan, who makes no move to leave. I give him a look.

He eyes me from head to toe. "What? It's nothing I haven't seen before."

"And it's nothing you're ever going to see again." I twist my index finger to indicate he needs to turn around. He grunts, but obeys.

Once I'm finished, Ryan and I wait in the small room without saying anything else. He looks skeptically at the speculum sitting on the counter while I try to get comfortable, the stupid paper coverings making obnoxiously loud crinkling sounds.

After what feels like hours, there is finally a knock at the door before the doctor walks in, introducing herself. "Hi Kelley, I'm Doctor Conners. Let's see what we've got going on in here, shall we?" She points to my stomach, smiling at both Ryan and I excitedly.

Glancing at my chart, she starts to go over some of my information, confirming things like my age, the fact I don't smoke, and the date of my last period. Ryan smirks, enjoying this way too much, and just when I think the personal questions are over, Dr. Conners studies the chart more closely. "And I see here that you had a miscarriage about seven years ago?" Her voice gets soft and she looks at me sympathetically. Ryan's smile immediately fades. I'm not sure how to read the expression that passes over his features, so I avoid eye contact and simply nod.

Thankfully Dr. Conners doesn't ask anything else, and proceeds to wash her hands, put on a pair of gloves, and grab a bottle of gel from the counter. She motions for Ryan to stand beside me and has me scoot down as she lifts a wand attached to a cord, slathers on some lube, and ducks her hand under the drape. She fiddles with a few knobs on the cart next to her with her free hand, adjusting a small screen so that both Ryan and I can see.

After a few painfully long, silent moments a black and white blob flickers onto the screen. It looks like nothing but splotchy shadows, but it instantly captivates me. Ryan shifts closer to get a better look.

It's in this moment that I feel an odd mixture of joy and

sadness. Up until now this life inside me felt somewhat abstract or intangible, like the doctor might say, *"Pregnant? No way. You just need to lay off the cheeseburgers."* But now I see, in plain black and white, just how real this really is. Jake and I never got to see an ultrasound before I lost the baby, and I realize that may have been for the best. I'm overcome by such a sense of wonder that I am now solely responsible for growing, raising, and protecting an entire person that I'm terrified by the thought something bad might happen. And when I realize just how lonely it will be not to have someone who loves me to share this with, I feel a sharp sting in my throat.

I feel Ryan's fingers brush against my shoulder. The way he drapes his arm over the back of the table is so damn casual it might be accidental, but I'm grateful for the contact. It brings me back to the present moment so I can focus on what Dr. Conners is saying.

"Hope you don't mind a Spring baby. It looks like you're due May 9th. Everything else is looking good so far, so we'll schedule you for your next appointment in about five to six weeks." She removes the wand and her gloves before handing Ryan and I each a small, printed picture. I see Ryan casually slip his into his back pocket. The doctor lets me know I can get changed before she exits the room. Ryan pauses before gesturing toward the door. "I guess I'll wait for you out there."

I nod, and once he leaves I allow myself a brief moment to stare at the picture in my hand. I wipe a single tear that's slid down my cheek before tucking the photo into my purse and standing to get dressed.

CHAPTER

six

Ryan

THE DRIVE BACK TO KELLEY'S place is quiet. I put the car in park and, without saying anything, open the passenger door and follow her into the building. Once inside her apartment she puts her keys and bag on the kitchen counter as I lean against the opposite side.

Neither of us know what to say, so I decide to break the ice. "How come you didn't tell me?"

Kelley lets out a deep breath, not needing an explanation of what I'm talking about. "What's the point? It was a long time ago."

I can tell she has so much sadness pent up inside her that I should drop it, but I fucking want to know more. "Is that why you haven't had a relationship all this time?"

She hangs her head, looking ashamed. "No. Not exactly."

Jesus, this is like pulling fucking teeth. "Is it why you and your ex broke up?" A disgusting thought flashes through my mind. "Did he fucking hurt you?"

She looks at me, no doubt surprised by my lack of tact. But some sick feeling in the pit of my stomach has it twisting in knots, so I need to know what happened. I don't know if it's because I actually like this chick as a friend, or because I just saw my kid in her uterus, but I am overcome with such a fierce sense of protectiveness I'm ready to beat the ever living shit out of anyone that's touched her. Thankfully she relieves my worst fears. "No, Jake never hurt me. Not physically, anyway. He and I were over long before the baby; I just didn't want to admit it. He wasn't right for me and I knew it. Fate knew it, too."

She whispers that last part and I want to shake her. What the fuck does fate have to do with it? Does she really believe she was being punished or some shit? "You really believe fate had any goddamn say in what happened?"

She shrugs. "I'm just saying I wasn't honest with myself—or Jake—about our relationship back then and everything went to hell. I know I'm never going to make that mistake again, which is why I want us to know where we stand with each other."

I don't know how to respond to that, so we're both quiet again before Kelley stands up straighter and clears her throat. "I've been thinking about what we should do, and I don't think we have to tell anyone you're the father."

Back to this. I fix her with a hard stare. "I thought I made it clear I'm not going anywhere."

She looks uncharacteristically nervous and refuses to make eye contact. "I'm not saying you can't be involved somehow, I'm just saying other people don't have to know about it."

"I'm not going to keep the fact that this baby is mine a big fucking secret. Weren't you the one just talking about being honest?" I can't help but let my past experiences with lies and abandonment and keeping shit hidden get the better of me. I'm not the type of guy to shirk his responsibilities, but even I didn't expect to feel such an innate sense of pride as soon as I saw that tiny blob on the screen. I may not know how to be a father, but I'm sure as hell going to try and figure it out.

Kelley regains her composure. "I'm just saying it might look bad—for both of us—if we admit we let this happen. I'm not thrilled about people knowing I'm pregnant to begin with, let alone who I screwed. It's not so much a lie as keeping our business private." When I refuse to break our gaze, she shrugs, defeated. "Come on Ry, you have to know what people will say about me if they knew. Everyone knows you've made it perfectly clear you don't do commitments or relationships so I'll just end up looking pathetic. I mean I've already ruined my shot at finding love anytime soon, but if I have any sort of hope for a future husband I don't want to have to explain I was stupid enough to get pregnant from a one night stand with the town's most unavailable bachelor. And I don't want our kid to grow up confused or teased, either. Since we're not together, it will be easier to keep our lives separate."

She looks sad and embarrassed, and fuck, it makes me feel like a complete and utter jackass. I know how hard I've worked to be open and clear about my relationships—or my intentional rejection of them—but Kelley shouldn't have to suffer because of that. If we keep this a secret I might get off easy, but she can't exactly hide her condition forever. She's not the kind of girl to act irresponsibly, and it's partially my fault for convincing her to loosen up in the first place.

Plus the thought of any other guy near her—near my kid—makes me feel a very fucking strange sense of jealousy.

Lucas' words about doing the right thing collide with the memory of my dad walking out, and before I have time to think

I blurt, "What if we tell people we're engaged?" As soon as the words come out I wish I could take them right fucking back. *Shit! Blake, you are a stupid fucking asshole.*

She looks as stunned as I feel at hearing the words explode like a fucking bomb from my mouth.

"What?" she asks, genuinely confused.

I shrug as if it's the easiest, most logical thing in the world, not letting on how much I doubt the shit I'm about to spew. "If we tell people we're together, it won't appear so reckless."

She contemplates this before slowly clarifying. "So you're saying we should pretend we're getting married and that's why we're having this baby? What was that about not wanting to lie?"

Now she sounds amused, and maybe somewhat intrigued. I smirk, despite feeling like a hypocritical douchebag. I'm sure as fuck not thrilled about lying, but at this point it seems like the best way to protect us all. I can already feel the fucking judgment of everyone thinking I'm just a deadbeat like my father who abandons his kid, nevermind the hell there'd be to pay if my mother knew I got a girl I barely know pregnant. Clearly she has a sore spot when it comes to irresponsible men who walk away from their problems. Forget the fact I've turned my life around and made something of myself—this would be all it takes for her to assume I'm just an asshole like my dad. Like father, like son, right? The fact I still even care one tiny bit about what that woman thinks makes me want to put my fist through a wall. The irony that I'm going to be just like her, lying to keep up appearances to gain the approval of others, is not lost on me. Except I'm doing this to protect my child, not to ignore it. "That's exactly what I'm saying. Besides, like you said it's our business, so what the fuck does it matter if we decide to keep the truth to ourselves? This is about doing what's right for us and the baby and it's nobody else's goddamn business."

Kelley shakes her head. "You're crazy, you know that. We already drive each other mad. And what happens down the road? I mean eventually the truth will have to come out."

I know she's right, but I can tell the idea appeals to her. Hell, I'm not sure how it will all work, but I know I refuse to come off as a dick abandoning his kid and I also know I don't want Kelley to go through this alone. If this will keep us both from looking careless, it's a win-win.

I lean against the counter, trying to explain. "Look, we might be coming at this for different reasons, but the fact remains that neither of us wants to look irresponsible. I don't want to come off as a douche just as much as you don't want to come off as a slut. Plus you're probably going to need help over the next few months, so we'll just tell people we fell madly in love, are getting married, and starting a big happy friggin' family. It will buy us some time to figure our shit out and after the baby is born and things settle we can stage a breakup. We'll say it didn't work out, but by that point we'll have established we were at least serious about each other when this happened so it won't seem so bad. Then I can still be in our kid's life without any questions." I nod confidently, trying to convey how rational this can be.

Kelley mulls that over before lighting up with a taunting smirk. "You know this would mean you can't have sex for over nine months, right?"

OK, maybe this is a worse idea than I thought . . .

Refusing to give in, I shoot her my own cocky smile. "Well since you're my fiancèe and all, I think we could work something out." I wink suggestively.

She shakes her head in disgust, but I notice her cheeks blush.

I can't resist riling her up. I experience some sort of sick pleasure when she gets fiery on me. "What? I've always used a condom and get tested regularly if that's what you're worried about." She rolls her eyes so I raise my eyebrow and add, "Hey, my junk is clean and you're already pregnant, so what else can happen?"

That actually makes her laugh, and I'm relieved to see her visibly relax.

The fact I'm sort of comfortable with the idea of pretending to be together makes me pause. I mean I'm about to tread in some pretty dangerous waters getting involved with such a big commitment, even if it is fake. Then again, this woman *is* carrying my child. It's justifiable I feel a primal need to protect her and make us both feel at ease. It doesn't have to mean anything more. Again, as long as we each know the deal going in, it should be easy.

Because that worked out so well the last time, didn't it, asshole?

Kelley gets serious. "If we're really going to do this we have to set some rules. We have to make this seem real if anyone is going to buy it."

I cross my arms. "Agreed."

"First, I'm serious about the no sex thing. I mean it, Blake. It would be beyond mortifying if someone thought you were cheating on me. A fake relationship is bad enough, but a fake betrayal would be the ultimate embarrassment. If there's a chance of that happening there is no point starting this."

I want to make a joke, but the look on her face tells me it wouldn't be funny. "I can be discreet."

She shakes her head. "Forget it. See, we're already in trouble. This whole idea is ridiculous."

She throws her arms up in defeat as she leaves the kitchen. I drop my head and put my hands in my pockets. I feel the edge of the small photo the doctor handed me, and instantly feel like a tool. I want to help her—help our child—and here I am, too selfish to give up sex for a few months. That's what got us in this mess to begin with, so I fucking should be celibate for a while.

I follow Kelley into the adjacent living room. She's laying with her arm over her eyes.

I sit on the back of the couch and let out a big sigh. "Fine. No sex."

She peeks out from under her arm, eyeing me doubtfully. "I refuse to be a burden, Ry. I don't want to change or ruin your life. This has to be completely mutual if it has any chance of working. I can justify lying to everyone else for the sake of our child, but we have to promise to at least be honest with each other."

She's just being real, which I respect. "This was my idea, remember? If us pretending to be together is best for our kid right now, I'll do whatever it takes. You're going to need help and I can certainly abstain for a few months. No biggie." Right?

She doesn't look convinced, so I know I need a way to prove I'm taking this seriously—to prove I'm not going anywhere. "In fact, you should move in with me."

If she looked confused before, now she looks downright baffled. Maybe even scared. "Me? Live with *you*?"

Good point. Fuck!

"We want this to be convincing, right?" I swallow down my own reservations, knowing if I take it back now I really am a dick. "Plus with our work schedules it will be easier to live in one place. And mine is bigger so it just makes sense." It's practical more than anything.

She can't argue with that. "Fine." She sighs and I smirk, feeling victorious for winning this debate, no matter how fucked up it might be. She stands up and heads for the kitchen.

Before she rounds the corner she turns around and calls over her shoulder, "But I get the bed. You're sleeping on the couch, buddy."

My smile fades.

What the hell have I gotten myself into?

CHAPTER

seven

Nine Weeks

Kelley

THE FRIDAY AFTER RYAN AND I come up with our crazy scheme, I pack a few bags after work and he's driving me to "officially" move into his apartment. I was definitely skeptical about this whole thing at first, but Ryan *did* make some valid points, even if I think he's doing it to save his own ass more than anything. As much as it goes against my idea of true love, in the end pretending to be together is the only way for us to get out of this without seeming completely careless. I realize the risk in getting too close when my emotions are going haywire as it is, but the selfish side of me really just wants someone around . . . even if it is Ryan Blake. Truthfully, I'm scared of being pregnant and alone. I can deal with the type of loneliness that forms while waiting for the right guy to come along, but bringing a kid into the picture by myself? I worry about something happening to the baby again, which sends me further into a panic. I push the thought from my mind.

It doesn't help that all week I've been having crazy ass intense dreams where I'm either held captive or drowning or being attacked and Ryan comes galloping in to save me, quite literally, on a white horse. I reassure myself that this situation has nothing to do with needing to be rescued—it's simply about doing what makes the most sense for our baby. Besides, how seriously can I take a dream where the villain has condoms for limbs?

Stupid pregnant hormones.

Ryan pulls his truck into the gated parking garage of an upscale apartment complex. Most lawyers I know tend to be well off, and Ryan is clearly no exception. He opens my door and helps me down before grabbing two of my suitcases. He grunts as he carries them, leading me inside the building. "Jesus, Brooks. What the hell do you have in here, bowling balls?"

I shrug innocently as we enter the lobby. A burly, bald man in a dark suit and tie is stationed by the front door, looking stern. When he sees Ryan a boyish smile transforms his ebony face. Ryan puts my bags down and grasps one of the man's big hands. They do that one-arm hug thing guys do as they slap each other's backs.

"B-man, how they hangin'?" The man punches Ryan playfully.

"Big D—everything's good. Did you have a nice vacation?" Ryan asks in return.

I try not to giggle at their nicknames before "Big D" notices me. "And who is this?" he asks, genuinely curious and obviously surprised.

Ryan looks at me hesitantly, but only for a second before he moves to my side and puts his arm tightly around me. "Darrin, I'd like you to meet my fiancée, Kelley. Kelley, this is Darrin, head honcho in charge of security. It's his job to keep the crazies out."

I try to look lovingly at Ryan and wrap my arm around his waist. I can feel his strong, muscular frame beneath his shirt so my lust isn't exactly hard to fake.

If Darrin isn't convinced about us as a couple, he's too polite to show it. He grabs my hand while saying, "Well, well. Look who finally got this guy to settle down. I've known him for eight years and I always wondered when he would find a girl special enough to let upstairs."

I'm puzzled by Darrin's odd comment, but before he can elaborate Ryan interjects. "Darrin, since Kelley is moving in with me I'm going to need another key for her. She also has a red Honda that will need access to the garage. I know you'll hook us up." Ryan claps Darrin's arm in a way that indicates there is no need for further discussion. At least I assume that's what the strange look that passes between them is about. Darrin says he'll take care of it as Ryan thanks him and grabs my things. He gestures toward the elevators and I follow him over. When the doors ding open we both step inside. Ryan pushes a button and the metal slides closed.

I stare at Ryan curiously before asking, "What did Darrin mean about you finally letting someone upstairs?"

His right shoulder bobs up and down. "Who knows. Probably just making small talk. He's a good guy. If you ever need anything when I'm not here, you can count on him."

When we get up to the fifth floor, Ryan unlocks the door labeled E4.

Based on the lobby alone I should have expected the apartment to be impressive, but my jaw drops when I walk inside.

To the left is a galley style kitchen with dark cherry wood

cabinets and black granite countertops. A bar height counter flanks the right, with a few stools on the opposite side. Directly ahead is a spacious living room with a ginormous L shaped leather couch and matching recliner. A big, dark wooden coffee table is in the center of the room. A huge flat screen tv is mounted on the wall. Behind the couch is a dining area, consisting of a black table and six matching chairs. Ryan points to the left beyond the kitchen, indicating a short hallway leading to the bedroom, which he says also includes a walk-in closet and master bath. He points to the hallway off to the right, noting that's where the guest bathroom is.

I follow him around, taking a quick peek at everything as he gives the short tour. While there aren't a ton of rooms, the place feels huge and open. It's minimalist in style, but oddly comfortable. My apartment is filled to the brim with pictures and books and souvenirs. I think the more stuff I have to remind me of the places I've been and people I've known, the more it feels like home. Funnily enough, Ryan's place has virtually none of these things, but still feels safe and cozy.

I notice a doorway at the very end of the hall past the guest bath.

"What's in there?" I nod toward the half-closed door.

"That's my office. I'm pretty obsessive about my workspace so I usually keep it closed off." He pushes the door open so I can peek inside. I see a big, expensive looking desk and a dark red tufted leather office chair. Framed certificates and awards are placed perfectly on the walls, a bookshelf filled with pictures, knick-knacks, and trophies sits opposite the desk. It's obvious this is the only room Ryan puts all of his personal touches on so it must mean a lot to him.

"You're welcome to do whatever to the rest of this place, but this room is off limits. I need some sort of manly sanctuary if you're going to start burning incense and hanging pink fuzzy curtains or whatever other girly shit you have planned." He closes the door and steers me back to the bedroom, placing my suitcases in the corner of the room. "I cleared some space in the closet for you. I'll sleep on the couch so you can have the bed, as promised."

I run my finger along the white down comforter lining the king sized bed. I plop down, stretching out my arms. "Considering your couch is about as big as this bed, I don't feel sorry about it."

He chuckles as he grabs something from one of the bedside table drawers. "I thought you should wear this. You know, to make our story believable."

He holds a small, shiny object between his fingers. I stare at the diamond ring, then at his face. He looks like his usual, mellow, unaffected self.

I've pictured being proposed to many times in my life, but never was it as unceremonious as this. I know it's not real, but I can't help but feel sad about it.

Rather than let Ryan know this, I choose instead to give him a hard time.

"Really? That's the best proposal you could come up with?" I cross my arms teasingly.

He rolls his eyes, but next thing I know he's dropping to one knee in front of me, holding out the delicate jewel.

"Kelley Sunshine Brooks, will you do me the honor of being my fake fiancée?" A giant, cheesy smile spreads across his face as he grabs my hand.

I can't help but laugh at his overly dramatic display as he slides the ring on my left ring finger. I also try not to notice how perfectly it fits.

Ryan quickly pulls back before getting up and heading to the closet that leads to the bathroom. He grabs a blanket and pillow from the top shelf. "I'll leave you to get settled then. If you need anything, let me know."

I nod appreciatively as he leaves the room and closes the door behind him.

I take the opportunity to look at the ring sparkling on my hand. Again, not exactly how I pictured this going down, but I must admit Ryan's taste in jewelry is impeccable. Two small diamonds flank a larger princess cut one in the center of a classic setting. There is something stunning about it's simplicity. I begin to picture him making a special trip to a jewelry store, telling the clerk how he needs something perfect for the love of his life.

Yeah. Right.

He probably picked it up at Walmart on his lunch break and I'm sure it was cheap. It's probably not even real. The realization makes my throat feel tight, but I shake it off. I'm just tired. It's been a long day and I can barely keep my eyes open. I quickly change into some comfy pajamas—a pair of shorts and an old t-shirt—before unpacking my toiletries. I wash my face and pee for the bajillionth time today. As I brush my teeth, I'm entertained by how neat and meticulous everything in the bathroom is. Maybe I expected some dirty, smelly bachelor pad, but I am pleasantly surprised by the tranquil vibe of Ryan's place. It's very much a reflection of his personality, and I find it reassuring.

I shuffle over to the bed and slide down between the sheets. I've never felt so small in a bed before. I can fully stretch out in every direction and not even come close to the edge. I curl up on my left side and hug one of the pillows tightly to my chest. It smells like cinnamon, and that's the last thing I remember before drifting peacefully off to sleep.

I'm woken up by the same smell of cinnamon, which is now

overpowering. I feel a warm, firm body pressed against mine as a tongue expertly glides across my chest, sending thrills of pleasure down my spine. I run my fingers through the man's hair and pull his face to kiss mine. At the same time I feel him push his big, hard length deep inside me and I unashamedly moan into his mouth. He tastes delicious. He nibbles my ear before whispering, "Mine. You're all fucking mine." I open my eyes and see two dark blue ones staring wildly back at me. I've never felt so much pleasure in all my life. My head falls back against the pillows in complete ecstasy. He pounds into me so fast and hard I'm afraid he will split me in two. But it feels so good I don't really care. Just as he sends me careening over the edge, I cry out "Ryan!" loudly and passionately before I lose all consciousness.

Suddenly I'm running through a dark forest, being chased by someone wearing all black. The wind is howling and whipping around my face while leaves crunch loudly under my feet. I'm running as fast as I can, but every time I glance over my shoulder he's right there, only a few steps behind. My heart is pounding and I can barely breathe. I trip over a fallen tree branch and fall to the ground with a sickening thud. I try to scramble away, but a jolt of excruciating pain spreads through my ankle. I feel a heavy hand grip my shoulder. I try to scream as the man pulls me up roughly to face him . . .

I jolt upright, sweaty and short of breath. It takes a second for me to realize where I am.

It was just a dream, Kell. A super sexy fantasy turned super scary nightmare, maybe, but a dream all the same.

It just felt so goddamn vivid and real. I can't tell if the dampness of my shorts is from sweat or desire, but the way my heart is racing and I feel extremely on edge makes me want to run and wake Ryan up. I never got to see the creepy man's face, which makes it even more terrifying. The lights outside are casting strange shadows on the wall, making my skin crawl. I take a few deep breaths and just as I'm starting to calm down a gust of wind rattles the windows, scaring the ever living shit out of me.

Fuck this.

I scramble out of bed and scurry to the living room where Ryan is asleep on the couch. He looks completely content, lying on his back with his left arm outstretched above his head. The way his chest moves lazily up and down tells me he's out cold. I slide quietly next to him. As I shimmy my way under the blanket, pressing my body to his so as not to fall off the edge, my hand brushes against something warm and muscle-y. And semi-hard.

Ryan stirs and stares at me through confused, half-awake eyes. "Brooks? What the hell are you doing?" His voice is rough and raspy . . . aka hot and sexy.

I unceremoniously blurt out "You sleep naked?"

He exhales a gravelly chuckle, lightly tugging at the hem of my t-shirt. "If I knew you were planning to sleep with me, I would have told you the dress code." I poke him in the ribs, which makes him twitch. "Hey, you're the one who woke me up. Is everything OK?" he asks in a sleepy voice.

I tuck the blanket closer to my legs, creating a barrier between our lower halves. "I had a bad dream. These stupid pregnancy hormones make everything seem so real and your room is too big and quiet. It's creepy."

Ryan goes still and for a second I think he fell back to sleep. He leisurely rolls over and drapes his arm over my midsection, his fingers splayed across my stomach. Before he drifts off he slurs, "I'll keep you both safe, Sunshine."

When his breathing slows I know he's fallen back into a deep slumber.

I, on the other hand, lay wide awake for another hour, trying not to read too much into his words. The less I try to attach meaning or feeling to this situation, the easier it will be.

Once I finally succumb to sleep, I slip easily back into dreaming about a certain body part situated beneath the thin covers next to me.

CHAPTER

eight

Ryan

I'M SURPRISED TO WAKE UP with a warm, soft body sprawled over mine. I vaguely recall a conversation with Kelley late last night that I thought was a dream. Apparently not.

Her hair is tangled and messy. Her cheek is on my chest. I feel a hot burst of air as she breathes in and out. On every exhale an adorable, muffled snore escapes. I instinctually hug my arms tighter around her. When she melts into my arms, wrapping her leg around mine, my dick springs to life. That's enough to snap me fully awake and realize this is a bad idea.

A very *bad idea.*

Rule Number One for Keeping Control: remove temptation. Here I have a gorgeous girl—who happens to be carrying my child—living in my apartment—which is a big fucking deal in itself—wearing nothing but a thin t-shirt and short shorts, cuddled against me as my cock threatens to bore a hole right through the blanket. And I agreed to stay celibate for the next nine months. What the fuck was I thinking?

I maneuver myself out from under the covers and rise off the couch. Kelley starts to move, and I freeze like a fucking deer caught in big, beaming headlights. She settles back down, hugging the pillow in my absence. I take the opportunity to sprint my naked ass to the bedroom. I need some damn pants. And a cold shower.

A short time later I'm clean and calm and walk back to the kitchen wearing a pair of jeans and an old college t-shirt. Kelley is no longer on the couch, but I hear water running in the spare bathroom so I start messing around in the kitchen.

By the time Kelley exits the bathroom and walks over to sit on one of the stools, mumbling a groggy, *"Morning,"* I'm topping off two mugs.

"Morning. Sleep well?" I can't resist a seductive smirk. She rolls her eyes and I let out a quick chuckle. "I thought we'd have some breakfast and then go to your place to get your car and the rest of your things."

"Sounds like a plan."

I extend one of the mugs and she reaches for it eagerly. "Ah, bless you." She goes in for a big sip. As soon as the liquid reaches her mouth, she nearly spits it out. She manages to choke it down, but sticks out her tongue afterwards. "This is the weakest coffee I've ever had."

"That's because it's tea." I lean back against the counter, taking my own sip.

"Seriously? No coffee?"

"I don't drink it, but even if I did I wouldn't give you any. I read caffeine isn't good for pregnant women. This stuff has ginger or some shit in it, which is supposed to help if you feel sick." I might have been bored a few nights this week and stumbled across some baby forums online. Sue me.

"I feel sick all right . . ." Kelley rests her chin in her hands. "So, no alcohol and no caffeine. Now I can understand why you gave me such a hard time about *Grind*. What's your deal, Blake? Are you some sort of health nut?"

I shake my head. "I just prefer not to indulge in addictive behaviors."

"That's gotta take some crazy willpower."

"Nothing sacrificed, nothing gained." I reach in the cabinet. "Here. I also picked these up for you. I heard it's a good brand." I place a plastic bottle on the counter between us.

She picks it up and stares at me accusingly. "Don't tell me you're going to be one of *those* guys."

I raise an eyebrow. "Those guys?"

"You know, the kind who thinks that just because half your DNA is inside my uterus, you have a right to dictate what I can and can't do." She slams the bottle filled with prenatal vitamins back on the counter before crossing her arms angrily.

"Jesus, Brooks. I'm just trying to be helpful. Forget the vitamins if they offend you that much." I pick up the pills to throw them in the trash. Can't a guy do something nice without getting his head ripped off? I read about mood swings, but shit, it's going to be a long nine months.

Kelley lunges across the counter to grab my elbow. "Wait, Wait. I'm sorry. I'll take them." She slides the bottle from my hands and sits back on the stool. We stare at each other in an awkward silence before she gestures to the carton of eggs on the counter behind me. "I believe you mentioned something about breakfast? Remember, I'm eating for two now. And I plan to take full advantage of that."

I return her playful smile, confused by her emotional one-eighty, but fucking relieved she's no longer upset. For now.

"Coming right up, Sunshine."

Yup, it's definitely going to be a long nine months.

Eleven Weeks

"TELL ME AGAIN WHY WE agreed to do this?" Kelley frowns as she grabs the foil-covered apple pie she made that's sitting on the dashboard as I hold open her car door.

"Because Lucas and Eli are family and I always spend Thanksgiving here." I extend my arm to help her down from the truck. "Plus Luc fucking blackmailed me into it."

I slam the door closed and we make our way to the door. "Do you think Eli knows the truth?" The hesitation in her voice is apparent.

"Nah. Luc might give me shit but he's true to his word." Both Lucas and Kinsley know about the baby, but as soon as we told them about us moving in together they knew the whole engagement thing was a crock of shit. We swore them to secrecy, though, so as far as I'm concerned nobody else should ever need to find out. We're waiting until she's further along to tell anybody else she's pregnant—Eli included—so today is basically going to suck.

I let us in the back door at Eli's house, not needing to knock. He has always been like a father to me and I hate to fucking keep secrets from him, but it's all just part of the goddamn mess I've gotten myself into.

As we enter the kitchen Eli and Kinsley are sitting at the table talking while Luc leans against the counter nursing a beer. Eli looks genuinely thrilled as he gets up to greet us. He hugs me and then Kelley before saying, "I hear congratulations are in order, huh?"

Kelley eyes me nervously but plasters on a big smile for Eli. We both nod stiffly. I silently remind myself he's only talking about the engagement, but it doesn't help that Lucas gets the biggest shit-eating grin on his face and I have to resist flashing him a certain hand gesture. Suddenly Kelley thrusts out her hands and practically shouts, "I made pie!" causing everyone to stare at her outburst. Kinsley not so subtlety hops up to cause a distraction by hugging Kelley. Thankfully Eli doesn't acknowledge something weird is going on and thanks Kelley for the pie before putting it on the counter for later.

I turn to greet Lucas and as we shake hands he leans in and grunts, "Way to play it cool, bro."

I scowl at him, feeling jealous for the first time in a very long time that he's holding a beer right now. Today is obviously going to be awkward as fuck.

When we sit down to eat and get caught up with our usual small talk, I finally relax. Lucas and I dig each other at every chance we get while Kelley and Kinsley laugh and roll their eyes. It feels comfortable to have everyone joking and shooting the shit.

Once we've all had our fill of turkey, stuffing, and Eli's famous sweet potato casserole, Eli gets a big smile on his face. "You know, for as long as I can remember it's just been me and these two knuckleheads around for the holidays." He gestures with his thumb to Lucas and me. We smirk innocently. "But I have to say it's quite nice to have the company of two such smart, beautiful ladies for a change. Ever since Luc and I lost his mom this house has been missing the sweet sound of a woman's laughter, and hearing it tonight makes this place feel like it's home to a real family again. I just want to say how lucky I am that my boys here found such perfect people to love and to spend the rest of their lives with." He holds up his water glass to toast. "Here's looking forward to many, many more years filled with moments like this."

A heavy, sentimental silence fills the air as everyone nods and follows suit. I try to swallow past the lump that forms in my throat before raising my own glass. The conversation between everyone else picks up again but the room suddenly feels too stuffy for me, so I excuse myself, mumbling something about grabbing dessert.

Once I reach the kitchen I place my hands on the counter, palms down, trying to take deep breaths. Lucas and Eli are pretty much the only family I have—the ones that have always been there for me anyway—and hearing Eli talk about his wife and Kelley and love and the future does weird shit to my head. And my chest. Love? That shit is just a sign of weakness. A sign you've lost control to someone else. But there is also nobody I respect more than Eli, and I realize I'm fucked if I think I could ever be anywhere close to the kind of father he is.

I hear a throat clear behind me and it just about makes me jump out of my skin. "Need any help with that pie?"

I glance back and relax when I see it's not Eli. Or Kelley. Neither of them need to know how fucked up I'm feeling about this right now. "Jesus, Kins. You scared the shit out of me." I laugh, but it comes out hollow.

"Sorry. Just thought you could use some help." She leans on the counter next to me. "And I'm not just talking about the pie." I raise my eyebrow confused. "It's weird to hear Eli talk about family, especially when you have such a messed up past like me." She smiles gently, and I think I know where this is going. "I get the sense you know how that is, too, Ry, right?"

I scoff like I have no idea what she's talking about. "I'm fine, Kinsley, really." Shit. What is it with everyone today? Maybe I can sneak out the back to avoid dealing with any of them.

She shrugs, seeming to buy it. "Ok." She reaches over and grabs the apple pie I've been staring blankly at. "But I used to think I could control everything, too, you know. It didn't work out very well for me, and I'm guessing it won't for you, either." She chuckles playfully before waltzing back to the dining room as if she didn't just try to call complete bullshit on me.

CHAPTER

nine

Fourteen Weeks

Kelley

FOR THE NEXT FEW WEEKS Ryan and I live like hermits, working overtime to avoid everyone. It's still too early to tell people I'm pregnant, and it's too weird to pose as a couple in public. We agreed to wait until my next ultrasound, which is this morning, before saying anything about the baby. Part of me has been scared something might happen, and part of me just isn't ready to deal with it. I've stalled as long as I can, as if my situation might magically make any kind of sense, but I'm starting to show and can't keep it hidden much longer. The less my clothes fit, the more I feel suffocated.

It doesn't help that Ryan and I have fallen into a comfortable, easy routine. One that lulls me into a false sense of security.

Sure, we still argue like crazy, but that's just us. As much as we disagree, we're actually quite similar.

Sometimes, like when I'm pigging out on ice cream watching eighties movies late at night, and Ryan keeps stealing bites from my spoon (even though he claims he doesn't want any) and I am overcome with a feeling of complete satisfaction and contentment, I have to remind myself that this isn't real. It might be how I pictured my life on the surface, but deep down this situation is only temporary—and completely messed up. I knew going in this is what I signed up for, though, so I keep on pretending, just like we agreed.

I wake up five minutes before my alarm and quietly slip out of bed, careful not to wake Ryan. After four straight nights of nightmares when I first moved in, I decided we could share the bedroom—as long as he keeps some damn pants on. The king bed is big enough that we don't have to touch, though somehow we always wake up right next to each other. It made sense at the time, but lately my sex drive has been increasing by the minute. That, coupled with my raging mood swings, makes for real fun times.

I take a long shower, letting the hot water calm my nerves. I'm anxious to see our baby blob on the ultrasound screen today. Nervous as all hell that something might go wrong, but excited.

I turn off the water and go to step out when I see it—a giant fucking spider blocking my way. I *hate* spiders. I instinctively scream and push myself back into the corner of the shower as far as I can. The bathroom door suddenly bursts open and a fierce, disheveled looking Ryan comes barging in.

"What the fuck? Are you ok?" He looks around wildly, fists clenched and ready, no doubt searching for the axe murderer my over-dramatic screams must have led him to believe was attacking me. When he realizes nobody else is here, he looks confused.

I try to cover myself as best I can with my hands and nod to the shower door just as the eight legged beast starts to crawl away. "There! Kill it! Before it gets away!"

Ryan holds the shower door open and squints at the floor. "Are you kidding me, Brooks? A fucking spider? That's why you're in here screaming bloody murder?"

I try to scoff indignantly, but the creepy crawly sonofabitch is on the move again making me shriek. "Please just get it!" I cower in the corner while Ryan grabs a wad of toilet paper.

He tries to squish it when it darts out from under him, making its way between Ryan's legs. I yelp as Ryan swears and hops around, trying not to step on it with his bare feet. "Fuck you, you little bastard. Ah, shit! Goddamnit!"

Ryan stubs his toe before launching himself to the ground, barely getting his hand down fast enough to squash the spider beneath the toilet paper. He balls it up and forcefully throws it in the toilet, as if slam dunking a basketball. He flushes and as the water swirls around he extends both his middle fingers to the bowl. "Take that you little shit."

Now that I know the spider is dead and can regain my composure, I can't help but laugh at how completely ridiculous this situation is. I hold my hand to my mouth to stifle the giggles, forgetting I'm completely naked until Ryan turns and eyes me lustfully through the glass.

I quickly move to cover myself again. "Ok. You can leave now."

Ryan crosses his arms and leans against the outside shower wall, facing away but making no move to actually leave. "Really. That's the thanks I get for saving your life?"

I try to keep the smile out of my voice. "Nice try. That peek is the only thing you'll get, so enjoy it, pal. Now get out please."

"Well since you said please . . ." He heads to the door, but before he exits he turns his head to get one last look. I reach for the nearest object—a sopping wet washcloth—and hurl it at him. "Go!" I yell, just as the cloth misses his head when he slips outside and closes the door, laughing the whole time.

By the time I exit the bathroom a half hour later, fully dressed and ready, Ryan is no longer in the room. I pad out to the kitchen and find him looking at his phone. He smiles as he pours me a mug of ginger tea, which I kind of enjoy now.

I grab a yogurt from the fridge and try to open the counter drawer to get a spoon, but it's stuck. I pull harder, frustrated.

Without saying a word, Ryan leans over the counter and flicks his finger to release a bit of plastic stuck inside. He casually goes back to what he was doing.

I remain still, looking puzzled. He glances up. "I couldn't sleep last night and installed some baby-proofing stuff around the house."

I pin him with an open-mouthed stare as I try to understand. "Is that what was in all those packages you've had delivered lately?" I grab a spoon from the newly opened drawer and point it at my belly. "You do realize this thing is the size of a lemon right now, right? I don't think it will be reaching for kitchen drawers anytime soon." He shrugs and returns to his phone.

I stroll to the living room to eat my breakfast, attempting to conceal a smile. I shouldn't find this adorable . . . I mean, he's crazy. I take a spoonful of yogurt and swallow it. I simultaneously try to swallow any feelings that make my heart want to melt. What right does he have doing cute shit like this? The guy needs to lay off the Internet research. I guess it's nice he's interested in helping and all, which is the point of me being here, but baby-proofing isn't necessary for our charade—especially this early—so what kind of crap is he trying to pull? I bet he's trying to mess with me . . . mock the fact that this is all a big joke. The thought makes me instantly angry.

"By the time our kid is old enough to get into things, this whole pretend family thing will be long over, anyway," I call from the couch, simultaneously trying to remind myself while also attempting to get a rise out of him as pay back. "Way to go wasting your time and money on that one, pal."

I can't tell if he doesn't hear me or purposely doesn't respond. Either way I'm left to sulk, feeling lonely and upset.

CHAPTER

ten

Ryan

"FAVORITE MOVIE?"

"Some princess bullshit."

"Real nice. It's called The Princess Bride. Favorite music?"

"Anything by Justin Bieber?"

"You really suck at this game, Blake."

Kelley rolls her eyes as she looks out the passenger window. We're on our way to her doctor's appointment, and for some reason she feels the need to test how well I know her. Something about making sure we're convincing as a couple. Like a stranger will ask whether or not I know her favorite food while we're waiting in line at the grocery store or some bullshit.

It's macaroni and cheese, by the way . . . the kind that comes shaped like cartoon characters. She eats that shit by the truckload.

I'm just happy she's not *actually* upset anymore. I stopped and got her a strawberry milkshake, because that's just what you do when you have a pissed off pregnant chick in your truck. That made her go from being the "Ryan is a complete douche who is ruining my life for real" type of mad to the normal "Ryan is pissing me off because he's an adorable asshole" kind of mad. I'll take the latter every friggin' time. It's one thing to provoke her as a joke, but it's another to truly screw up. I can't stand to see that sad fucking look in her eyes, especially if I put it there. How was I supposed to know she was going to get all moody because of some fucking baby-proofing? I may be jumping the gun, but since I have no goddamn clue about all of this responsible parent shit I figured it's best to get a head start. I'm also fully fucking aware our situation is temporary, which is why it pisses me off when she uses it as ammunition. Just because we aren't together for real doesn't mean I won't have my kid over all the time as she grows up. Or he. I could be down with either. As long as it's healthy and happy, I don't care if it's an alien.

I pull into a parking space outside the Health Center. "Like anyone really gives two flying fucks if I know you listen to Adele when you're upset." I put the car in park and remove my keys from the ignition.

Kelley pauses mid-sip. "How do you know that?"

"Because you get upset all the time."

Her eyes turn to daggers, but I hold my ground. "What? It's true. Even the mailman made you cry when he delivered someone else's catalog."

She looks like she wants to protest, but concedes. "OK, true. But since I'm going to have to push something the size of a watermelon out a hole the size of an olive in a few months, I think I get a free pass."

I nod in agreement. "Fair enough."

She smiles triumphantly, takes a final long sip from her

shake, unbuckles, and scoots out of the car.

A short while later Dr. Conners meets us in Exam Room Two where she squirts some goop onto Kelley's stomach. Thank God Brooks doesn't need to get undressed this time. I'm so keyed up from the no-sex rule that I'd probably get an uncontrollable boner like some horny fifteen-year old. Fuck, just seeing the bare skin of her stomach is enough to make me readjust. She's been wearing baggy clothes lately, but after this morning I finally got a chance to see the bump she's sporting. Damn it if it doesn't make me feel like a smug, proud bastard for some reason.

Dr. Conners plays with some dials on the machine when suddenly a distinct, rhythmic beating fills the room. I'm instantly hypnotized by the raspy measure. I hear the doctor mention something about a nice, strong heartbeat, but her voice is distant. Every other thought leaves my brain as each breath is commanded by the only sound I hear—the powerful and steady *thump-thump, thump-thump* of my baby's heart.

Our baby's heart.

Shit just got fucking real.

If I thought seeing the picture last time was enough to pull me under, hearing this has me fucking sunk.

A huge smile spreads across Kelley's face, making her light up. Her excitement is unmistakable. I know this shit won't be easy, but suddenly I have no doubts that I will do whatever it takes to take care of my child *and* the woman it's growing inside of. I make a silent vow to never, ever walk out on them. We might not be the most conventional family, but we'll make it work. Even after we end our fake engagement, I'm still going to be a part of their lives. I'm going to be a father.

The best motherfucking father EVER.

CHAPTER

eleven

Kelley

IT'S AFTER TEN P.M. WHEN I finally pull my car into the garage. I stayed late at work to make up for the lost time during my appointment this morning. I see Ryan's truck is already parked.

I enter the apartment to find Ryan with his laptop and some papers on the couch, dressed in sweatpants and a gray t-shirt. His long legs are outstretched, ankles crossed, resting on the coffee table. He's wearing his glasses, which really isn't fair. The man's not exactly hard on the eyes when he's wearing contacts, but something about seeing him relaxed in glasses adds an extra layer of hotness.

I plop my purse and keys on the kitchen counter and pull off my coat as he greets me. "Hey. I saved some pasta for you. It's in the microwave."

"Thanks—we're starving." I rub my stomach before pressing a few buttons to heat up the food. When it's done I grab the bowl and a fork and join Ryan on the couch.

He looks up from the computer screen. "How was work?"

"I told my boss I'm pregnant. He said not to worry about taking maternity leave, but I think he was secretly pissed." I shove a few pieces of ziti in my mouth. So good. I have to admit it doesn't suck living with a man who knows how to cook.

"Screw him. If you want to quit I can take care of things. You should be resting more, anyway. He's an ass for making you stay so late tonight."

I roll my eyes, hiding a smirk as I shake my head. How come he always manages to sound both protective and condescending at the same time? "I'm fine. You know I love my job. I finally got more responsibility and I'll prove I can still manage, even while I grow a human being. A few late nights aren't going to kill me."

He looks unconvinced, but surprisingly doesn't argue. He goes back to typing.

"What are you working on?" I ask, poking through some of the papers spilled next to me. As I slide a few papers around, I notice the corner of a small black and white photo clipped to a notepad below. Is that the ultrasound photo? Why the hell would Ryan Blake keep something so sentimental?

I move the rest of the papers to confirm. "What's this doing here?" I ask, puzzled.

Ryan glances at the photo and shrugs. "I like to keep it as a reminder."

"A reminder of what?" *The biggest mistake of your life?* A lump settles in my throat.

"A reminder that I have a chance to do something good in my life." Hearing something so profound catches me off guard. Ryan and I haven't talked much about how we feel, but something tells me hearing our baby's heartbeat this morning affected him just as much as it did me.

I stay quiet, not sure how to respond, while he takes the pile of papers, shuts his laptop and moves it all to his briefcase resting on the coffee table before changing the subject. "I have to ask you something."

He looks uncharacteristically nervous, which leads me to believe this is serious. I brace myself. "Yeah?"

He shifts to look at me, resting his elbows on his knees with his hands grasped in front of his chin. He lets out a big sigh, dropping his arms. "Will you meet my mom?"

I let out a laugh. "Seriously? That's it? Jeez, Blake. The way you're acting I thought it was something bad."

He leans back. "Clearly you know nothing about my mother."

I poke around what's left of my food. "Can't be worse than mine." I think of Ryan having to meet my own parents. He thinks my middle name is funny? Wait until he gets the entire Lila and Hal Brooks experience. I cringe at the thought.

"Seriously, Kell. My mother is completely whacked. I told her about us being engaged and the baby and she insisted we come to her holiday party next week. I can only imagine what kind of show she's going to put on. I'd try to get out of it but my sister, Hazel, and my grandmother really want to meet you. They're the only two family members I actually give two shits about. At least we can meet the whole big, happy fucking family in one shot and get it over with."

He looks genuinely agitated, which makes me feel bad. "I don't mind, Ry. Really. I figured this would have to happen at some point. I'm sure it won't be as bad as you think."

"I should warn you that my mother is manipulative. She may act nice and sweet, but it's bullshit." When I tilt my head questioningly, he explains. "Growing up things were hard. She practically ignored my sister and I after my dad left, which made us act out. She ignored that, too. I was lucky and got myself out of it, but Hazel is still stuck. I try to look out for her, which is why I'm civil, but know that if I could stop from throwing you to the wolves, I would."

I've never heard Ryan open up so much, so I take the opportunity to push further. "Stuck how?"

He pauses, and I'm afraid he's going to change the subject. He rests his head on the back of the couch before admitting, "When she was sixteen my sister got involved with a bad crowd and started using drugs. She was in really bad shape. I tried to talk some sense into her, but she wouldn't listen. I begged my mom to get her help, but she refused to acknowledge there was a problem. It got so bad dealing with things at home that I started to drink, and became a fucking alcoholic at the ripe age of seventeen. My sister got in some serious trouble and I was too shit-faced to stop it. A year later I hit rock bottom, went to rehab, and joined AA, thanks to Luc, Eli, and my Grams."

He grunts cynically and I suddenly feel very sad for him. Why he doesn't drink suddenly makes a lot more sense. It sounds like there's a lot more to this story, but I don't want to push it, so I settle for truthfully saying, "I'm glad you had people to help you."

"I owe them my life. Luc and Eli have always been there for me, and my grandmother did her best to make sure my sister and I were taken care of. My mom might be her daughter, but I could always tell Grams thought we deserved a better childhood. She secretly loaned me some money so I could get out of the house. It's then I started working three jobs and put myself through law school and paid her back. When I graduated I threatened my mom that she needed to finally get Hazel into rehab or I would start telling everyone the truth. Not wanting to risk a scandal, she did, and ever since has kept Hazel under her thumb. My sister not only relies on her for money, but she thinks she owes mom for saving her life and is too scared to leave."

Ryan looks tired, as if admitting all of this has completely drained him. He chuckles before adding, "See? Majorly fucked up."

I think back on all of the snap judgments I made about Ryan based on his laid back, unfazed demeanor. I stereotypically assumed he was just a pig, but now I realize he has good reason to be the way he is. I don't know if it's the hormones or what, but I feel the need to be close and slide over to him.

"Why wouldn't you tell her the truth?" I ask gently.

"Because I'm just glad she got better and has stayed clean for the past three years. If I tell her, things might go to hell again. Plus, it's my fucking fault she went through hell in the first place. If I had been there to stop it . . . well shit may have been a lot different."

The guilt Ryan feels is evident by the way his entire body slumps down, as if the weight of it all is literally too much for him to bear. I've never seen him look so vulnerable, and I want to comfort him. But I'm not sure how so I settle for saying, "Don't worry. We'll go to this party and meet everyone and it will be fine. I promise." I extend the pinky finger of my right hand and hold it out.

He looks at my finger skeptically. I roll my eyes and grab his left hand, hooking my pinky with his while smiling extra wide.

Our fingers and eyes remain locked for a long moment before he finally releases my hand and quickly stands up. "Time to call it a night. I'm beat." He heads toward the bedroom but turns before rounding the corner of the short hallway. He looks back at me with a small, unsure smile. "Goodnight."

I smile shyly back. "Night."

CHAPTER

twelve

Ryan

THREE HOURS LATER, I'M STILL awake. I glance at the clock. It's after one a.m. *Shit.*

This isn't going to work.

I slowly sit up—I heard Kelley come to bed a couple hours ago and I don't want to wake her. I swing my legs over the side of the bed to rest my feet on the floor. I look to my lap . . . I'm hard as a rock.

Fuck my life.

Hell fuck *anything*. I need to take care of this.

As I make my way to the bathroom and quietly shut the door I think about how I got myself into this mess. When I suggested Kelley move in, I surprised the hell out of both of us. I really thought I was keeping our kid's best interests in mind. You know, being helpful by not abandoning them both. Yes, it was also to keep myself from looking like a negligent asshole, but it was practical more than anything.

But now? I don't know who the fuck I am lately. I stare at my rattled reflection in the mirror. Baby-proofing? Sleeping in the same bed with an attractive woman night after night? Sharing stories about my past? I look down to my tented shorts. *Agreeing not to have sex?*

I feel like I'm going mad.

For ten years I've been extremely careful not to tempt myself with anything remotely habit-forming, but the more time I spend with Kelley, the more I fight that familiar pull. That undeniable, unforgiving addiction that pushes you to give in, even if you know it's wrong. First it was a bottle of strong liquor that promised the chance to forget my problems, and now it's a feisty, dark-haired girl that threatens to make me feel things I've worked damn hard to keep in check.

I never talk about my past, yet there I was tonight, spilling my guts right in front of her. *Because* of her. She's so goddamn understanding and easy to talk to it felt right. And hell, I even experienced some sort of relief finally getting it out. I thought, *Damn, it's nice to have a close female friend I can shoot the shit with.*

But then she had to look at me with those soft, serious, fucking beautiful eyes. My chest felt tight and my stupid dick decided it was time to leap into action and I knew I had to get away from her before I did something majorly fucking stupid.

I stalk to the shower and turn the dial to the left. I was a moron to think I could handle this situation. I just need to relieve this pent up tension and I'll be good to go.

I pull off my clothes and step behind the glass doors, letting the hot water pound the top of my head. I rest my hands against the cool glass in front of me, my head bowed to communicate some sort of sick prayer. I'm not a religious man, but I pray to anybody listening that I can maintain control these next few months.

Keeping my right hand on the wall, I grab my dick with my left and try to conjure any other woman's face in my mind. I try to put fifteen years worth of dirty magazines and porno videos to use and focus on anyone—*anything*—else.

It's no use. I squeeze my eyelids shut, trying to force my concentration, but all I see are two alluring eyes tempting me, challenging me. One is blue. One is brown.

I throw my head back, frustrated. I stroke faster, chasing a feeling of satisfaction that never comes.

I move to stand up straight. As I do, I catch sight of something to my left, just beyond the foggy shower door. For a second I think I'm imagining things, but I realize it's a curvy—very real—figure.

Two eyes stare lustfully back at me.

One is blue.

One is brown.

CHAPTER

thirteen

Kelley

YUP. I JUST WALKED IN on Ryan Blake masturbating in the shower.

. . . and I'm not even sorry about it. Thrilled is more like it.

I woke up to pee and this is what I accidentally walk in on. *Ah yes . . . there is a sex god!*

I can't help but admire the erotic sight when he notices me and we lock eyes.

I should leave. Turn around and run. Being around this man—fake fiancé slash overprotective father of my child—is becoming increasingly complicated. The more time we spend together, the more our clear cut lines defining this relationship begin to blur. I hate that I physically want him so badly—his warmth, his comfort, his touch—when I know I can't have him. Not in any real, meaningful way, that is.

But still, I can't look away.

"Can I help you with something, Brooks?" Ryan asks calmly, as if he's not standing there naked and dripping, holding himself.

The steam is providing a teasing cloud around him, allowing me to see enough to make my pelvic muscles clench. The water from the showerhead streams through his dark brown hair and down his face, pooling at his neck before sliding down the rest of his lean frame. A few droplets catch on his eyelashes . . . they splatter when he blinks them away. Completely forgetting the reason I came in here, I let my eyes roam his body, captivated by how *impressive* he is.

I lick my lips before softly admitting, "I think I'm the one that would like to help you."

He stares at me with a mixture of confusion and lust. We both freeze, wordlessly questioning the other. *Are we really going here?*

Finally, Ryan reaches for the shower door and pulls it open. His blue eyes remain fixed on me as his lip curls into a smirk. His cocky expression is both a challenge and a dare: *You won't do it, Brooks.*

For a second I almost give in to his silent taunt. This is a really bad idea. Except the thing about being pregnant is that all my senses are extremely heightened, and right now I am so turned on it makes me lose all rational thought.

The heat filling the room is making me feel deliciously dizzy. I peek to get a clear, full frontal view of Ryan and suck in a deep breath.

Damn it . . . I'M GOING IN.

Without any further hesitation I step boldly into the shower, our bodies pushed close in the small space. Still in my pajama shorts and tank top, they instantly get soaked. The thin fabric turns see-through, and by the way Ryan's eyes make their way to my swollen chest (which has grown a full size from my usual C cup), I assume he approves. He reaches for my waist and I slide my hands up his arms to feel his biceps. He grabs my ass and pulls me up against him, close enough to feel the hardness of his torso and legs . . . close enough to feel *all* of his hard parts. He smiles arrogantly, the same infuriating look he gets when he thinks he's won an argument, which makes me put my hand to his chest before he gets any closer. I sure as hell don't want him thinking he has the upper hand here.

"Just to be clear, Blake, this is only happening because being pregnant has turned me into some horny freak. You said you're clean and I know you haven't been with anyone for weeks, so I assume we're in agreement that this is just sex and means nothing else." I look at his face, trying to gauge his reaction. Maybe I'll admit there is some small part of me—a *very* small, insignificant part . . . more of a speck, really—that hopes I might see a touch of disappointment in his eyes. Not that I expect this to change things, but it'd be nice to know I might mean a little something more to him.

Except, as usual, he continues to look so goddamned neutral and sure of himself when he says, "Crystal clear, Brooks. Just sex." He grins, and I want to punch the look off his face. Or kiss it. Maybe both.

I start to lazily draw circles across his smooth chest with my finger, swirling the dripping water around and down his sculpted stomach until I reach just below his belly button. I look up at him seductively and add, "Good. I want to make sure it doesn't hurt your feelings if I'm only using you for my own pleasure." I admit that now I'm trying to provoke him. Two can play at this meaningless sex game. I don't want him nearly as much as he must need to get laid, right? He was the one in here jacking off after all . . .

I'm startled as he walks me back against the smooth glass,

pinning me so I can barely move. By the way my body automatically reacts, nipples hard and panties drenched, I know my plan has backfired. His left arm stretches out above my head as he runs his other hand slowly down the side of my face, past my neck, over my heaving chest, around the swell of my growing stomach, and under my shorts until his long fingers feel just how wet I am. I whimper as he leans in so that his mouth is dangerously close to mine. "At your service, Sunshine."

Next thing I know I'm angling forward so his mouth can land hungrily on mine. Without breaking away, he pushes my shorts and panties down my legs and pulls off my shirt. I run my fingers up and down his arms, noticing how strong they are. Solid. Determined.

His hands move to the back of my neck. We continue to kiss like mad. I grip his forearms, desperate for more. All of a sudden I feel a slight flutter in my abdomen . . . it feels like literal butterflies flying around in there. I pull back and look down at my round belly cocooned between our bodies. Damn it if the sight doesn't make something tighten in my chest. Ryan rests his forehead on my own and glances down, too. He gently places one of his large hands right at the top of my stomach before looking back at me. "Fucking perfect," he whispers before placing his lips roughly back on mine.

Before I have time to analyze if he means that in a complimentary or sarcastic way, I find myself surrendering. Every kiss, every touch is like fire to my skin. I ignite for him and not even the water pouring down around us can make it stop. I know I'm going to get burned, but that doesn't mean I can—or am willing to—prevent it.

He spins me around so my back is to his front. I press my palms to the wall for support. His hands travel my body and I feel his teeth scrape softly against the back of my neck. I push my ass into him, needing to feel just how much he wants this. By the way he growls in my ear, I'd say a lot. The man has been celibate for six weeks, after all. And right now I am more than willing to be the one he unleashes all that pent up sexual frustration on . . . I'm ready to spontaneously combust over here.

Thankfully I don't have to suffer his tortuous foreplay much longer because I feel him at my core, gliding to fit perfectly as he shifts to push inside me. I cry out in relief. I squeeze my eyes shut and let the warm water stream over me, glad he can't see my face—I don't need the smug bastard knowing exactly what effect he has on me.

As he drives in and out of me, he grips my hips so hard I'm sure I'll be branded with his fingerprints for days. The thought sends an extra ripple of excitement up my spine. I spread my legs and bend over, leveraging my weight against the glass. This steadies and intensifies each hard thrust. He snakes one arm around to rub my clit, making my knees weak. A moment later I feel the fire spread from my head right on down between my legs before rocketing up to settle in my chest. I come with a loud cry, and feel Ryan's own muscles contract simultaneously. We finish riding out the wave together before I feel him pull out and take a step back. I'm keenly aware of the stark emptiness I feel not having him still be a part of me.

After a few silent moments I cautiously look over my shoulder. Ryan coolly grabs the washcloth hanging on the small towel bar and starts to scrub himself, washing any evidence of what just happened down the drain. I bend down to grab my soaked clothes before turning around to face him.

"See, Brooks? Living together has its advantages." He smirks playfully.

I shrug indifferently. "I guess you're good for *something*." I try to remain casual, but a sudden shiver makes me tremble.

Ryan's brow furrows as he lightly rubs the goosebumps forming on my arms, this time keeping an arm's length distance between us. "You should grab a towel and get warmed up. I'll finish up in here and be out soon." He steps aside so I can get past him. I nod and do as he says, grabbing the first big white, fluffy towel I see, quickly covering myself.

I don't dare glance back as I scoot out of the bathroom, making sure to shut the door behind me. As I grab a fresh pair of pajamas and get into bed, I wait for the regret to creep in.

Except I can only picture him filling me, causing me to crave him all over again, even though he basically just gave me the brush-off. But did I really expect anything different?

I hear the water stop and a minute later Ryan, wearing a pair of shorts, turns out the light and crawls into bed next to me. He gets close, but not too close. *Damn.* After remaining quiet for a minute, he eventually says, "You know, Brooks, this situation is fucked up for the both of us, but if it had to happen, I'm glad it was with you."

He smells like soap, clean and masculine, and I have to resist rolling over to breathe him in. "And why's that?"

"Because you get me. You don't hide shit and you tell it like it is. I know I can trust you not to get all weird on me and we can have a mutual relationship where it doesn't have to be complicated or fucking filled with all types of drama. I respect that, and I respect you."

I slowly exhale the breath I didn't realize I was holding. I think I let my crazy, out of control emotions cloud my sanity for a second there. I take a minute to remember why I'm even here, in Ryan's bed—and in his life—in the first place. "I respect you, too, Ry. You didn't owe me anything after that night at the wedding, but I really do appreciate all you're doing for me. For us." I caress my stomach, suddenly aware of just how serious I am. "I still want a real family someday, but until I meet the right guy, it's nice to know I have you as a friend."

Ryan gets quiet and I wonder if he's fallen asleep. When he finally speaks the rawness of his voice surprises me. "I will always take care of you, Kelley. You and our baby. I may not be able to promise much else, but I can fucking promise you that."

I try not to notice how nice my first name sounds falling from his lips. It makes my insides feel funny, though. His words bring me an extraordinary amount of comfort, as I know he means them, but at the same time I feel that recurring emptiness when I think of how much I also want someone to love me. To be *in* love with me. I don't blame Ryan for this situation, I just wish it wasn't so complicated. For as much as we lay our cards on the table, I have a feeling we both still keep a few aces hidden up our sleeves.

I roll to my right side, facing him. Without any light I can barely make out his silhouette. While I'm not usually so shy, somehow tonight it's easier not to see his face. "I'm glad I'm having your baby, Blake, " I admit into the darkness.

And as we both fall asleep, I realize I wholeheartedly mean it.

CHAPTER

fourteen

Sixteen Weeks

Kelley

"DOES THIS DRESS MAKE ME look like a giant fat pregnant chick?" I step into the space between the living room and the kitchen where Ryan is waiting, feeling uncomfortable as I try to smooth the red fabric over my newfound curves. At five foot six with a lean frame, I feel like I'm showing way more than I should for being only sixteen weeks.

He eyes me from my simple black ballet flats, past the form fitting red dress that has three-quarter sleeves and falls just past my knees, all the way up to my face. I've left my long, brown hair down to fall past my shoulders and have applied a bit of makeup. I'm worried I look like I'm trying too hard to impress Ryan's family, but hell, I want them to like me.

Ryan's gaze lingers on my red lips for a beat longer before his eyes narrow. "Nice try, Brooks. I'm not walking into that fucking trap. You women all realize there is never a good answer for that kind of question, right?"

I cross my arms and pout. "The right answer is to say 'no,' ya big jerk."

He stalks over to me, looking mighty fine in dark jeans that hang on his hips in all the right ways, and a sexy, dark green button down shirt with the sleeves rolled up to reveal his cut forearms. He places his hands on my shoulders. "I hate to break it to you, Brooks, but you *are* a big, growing pregnant chick." He moves his hands down to my belly.

I punch him in the shoulder. Hard.

He flinches and retracts his arms. "Jesus it's a compliment!" I eye him fiercely as he tries to explain. "My kid is living in there and you are one cool ass woman to let him hang out in your womb for a while. Every day you get bigger, I know our baby is getting stronger and it's fucking hot." He smiles in such a damn arrogant, adorable way I have to laugh.

"Yeah, we'll see how hot it is when I have cankles and am too huge to be able to shave my legs anymore." I grin teasingly before turning to grab my coat.

He surprises me when he steps close to help me put it on. As he holds the thick wool up for me to slip my arms in, he responds playfully, "I could be into the whole cavewoman hippie thing." I snort before he says in a softer, gentler voice, "Seriously, you look great, Brooks. You always do, and you always will."

I blush as I fumble with the buttons on my jacket. For the past week and a half—ever since our steamy shower—Ryan and I have definitely gotten more comfortable around each other. While there is always an understanding that we're just friends, we now have a more physical relationship . . . shameless flirting, him rubbing and talking to my stomach, and yes, more sex. It may not be true love, but it's nice to have some semblance of a relationship going through all of this. It makes it easier to act like we're together when we genuinely like—and are attracted—to each other.

That doesn't stop me from being nervous about tonight, though. Ryan's whole family will be at the Christmas party, and from what he tells me there are always a ton of other people. At least Logan, Tristan, Kinsley, Lucas, and Eli will be there so I will know a few familiar faces. It will be the first time we're around everyone as an "engaged" couple, and I just hope we can pull it off. I try not to let Ryan pick up on my anxiety, because I know he is way more worked up about this than he is willing to admit. I could tell from the way he talked about his mom that this is the last place he wants to go, let alone also have to lie about our situation. I decide to keep things light to take his mind off it.

I pick up my small black clutch from the table and lightly swat his chest. "Well keep talking like that, mister, and you might just get lucky tonight." I wink as he chuckles and we make our way to the door.

Before I can pass him, Ryan holds his arm out to stop me and whispers in my ear, "What if I don't want to wait until tonight?"

Arousal spreads through my body, making me feel warm from the inside out. Before I have time to think of a witty comeback, he slaps my ass and says, "Come on, Sunshine. The sooner we get this shit over with, the better." He pulls open the door and motions toward the hall.

FORTY-FIVE MINUTES LATER WE PULL up to a ginormous, gated property. Ryan enters a code on the keypad and the gates start to move. As he pulls his truck up the long, winding drive, I can't help but literally let my jaw fall open.

"Jeez, Blake. I know you said your mom has money, but damn." I eye him curiously. "Are you sure you're not really Batman or something?"

He laughs as he puts the truck in park. "You caught me, babe. I'm wearing man tights under my pants as we speak."

I giggle at the thought. "Does that mean Lucas is Robin?" I laugh even harder picturing the two of them running around town in bodysuits, fighting crime.

"Fuck that. I work alone." He smirks, so genuinely happy it reaches his eyes, making them sparkle. I realize how proud it makes me to be the one to make him look that way. But all too soon he looks agitated again as he looks to the house, refusing to move or turn off the car. And *that* surprisingly makes me want to punch whoever hurt him in the past square in the face.

We sit in silence for a good minute and a half before I chance asking, "Soooo . . . are we going to go inside?"

He looks at me and wiggles his eyebrows. "Or we could have some fun out here." His usual cocky smile isn't completely convincing, and I know he's just trying to stall.

I grab his shoulder and shake it. "Come on, Blake. We're going in." He reaches for the hem of my dress but I swat his hand away and look at him firmly. "Now."

He hangs his head reluctantly but turns off the ignition. He takes two pieces of cinnamon gum out of his pocket and pops them into his mouth. Over the past few weeks I've noticed a pattern. When he's feeling relaxed he has one piece, and when he's feeling upset he has two. I find it curious and adorable. I've heard of people replacing one addiction with another, and it makes me wonder if chewing gum is a coping mechanism to help him stay sober.

As we each get out of the truck and walk up to the door he

grumbles, "For a fake fiancée you sure are bossy."

"Yeah, just imagine what I'll be like as a real wife someday. That will be someone else's problem. Lucky you dodged a bullet there, Blake, huh?" I try to laugh it off. I really did mean it as a joke, but for some reason the air shifts awkwardly between us. Before either of us can react, the big wooden front door swings open to reveal a slim, older woman wearing the fanciest beaded gown I've ever seen. "There's my baby boy!" She throws her arms around Ryan's neck and kisses both of his cheeks. He looks uncomfortable as he rolls his eyes and mumbles, "Hi, Mom."

The woman then turns her gaze on me and looks delightfully astonished. "And is this the girl carrying my grandbaby?"

Ryan puts a protective arm around my shoulder. "Mom, this is my fiancée, Kelley. Kelley, this is my mother, Holly Blake."

I smile, thankful Ryan's warm body is so close to mine. I'm trying really hard not to make any snap judgments, but for as sweet as this woman is acting there is still one serious icy vibe I'm getting.

She claps her hands together as she sizes me up, surely trying to gauge if I'm good enough for her son. "Well, Kelley, I'm so thrilled you're joining us. Now don't just stand there you two. Come in, come in." She ushers us into the house.

The entryway is gigantic and a huge, professionally decorated tree sits in the very center so it's the first thing you see when you step inside. People are milling about with drinks in their hands and waiters are carrying around silver trays of food. A beautiful girl with green eyes and aubergine hair runs up to Ryan and throws herself at him. He gets that genuine smile on his face again as he hugs her back.

"About time my favorite brother showed up to this thing." I notice the girl has the same exact teasing smile as Ryan, as well as a similar casual demeanor coupled with a cool edginess. She turns toward me and wraps me in a tight hug that feels natural and safe . . . the exact opposite of the impression her mother gives off. "And you must be the amazing girl finally tough enough to break this guy." She hooks her thumb at Ryan, who introduces us.

"Hazel, this is Kelley, and Kelley, this is my annoying sister, Hazel." Hazel sticks her tongue out at Ryan and he scowls, but I can tell they both adore each other. Neither of them seem anything like their mother, which amuses me.

Hazel looks at me and beams. "You're so pretty." She turns her head to look at her brother approvingly. "She's so pretty, Ry."

Ryan's eyes never leave mine as he answers, "Yeah, I know."

Hazel grabs my hands and looks at my stomach. "And oh my goodness, that's my little niece or nephew in there. I sure hope this kid takes after its mother in the looks department." She winks at me, indicating she's purposely riling Ryan up. I like this girl already.

Forgetting their mother is still here, I jump when I hear her voice right behind me. "For goodness sake, Hazel, let them come in and get settled. Be a dear and take their coats to the closet."

Hazel gives my hands a last squeeze before obeying her mother. Holly then comes between Ryan and I, putting an arm around each of our shoulders as she begins leading us into the adjacent room. "Your grandmother has been dying to see you."

As soon as we enter the living room an elderly woman calls out, "There he is!" in an excited tone as she hobbles over, using a cane for support. Ryan beams and takes a few quick strides to reach her first and envelops her in a warm hug. She holds on tight and looks just as thrilled to see him. I think back to when Ryan first talked about his grandmother and remember the appreciation that shone in his eyes. It's clear to me that they have a very special bond that is nothing like what he has with anybody else in his family.

The woman pulls back and places her hands on Ryan's cheeks. "You get more good looking every time I see you. Must take after me."

She winks and Ryan grunts, "You got that right, Grams."

She then notices me standing awkwardly behind Ryan and switches her focus. "You must be Kelley. You're even prettier than Ryan said." She hugs me and says, "I'm Gloria, but you can call me Grams." She pulls back to look at me and then taps Ryan in the chest with her cane. "You take care of this one, mister. I can tell she's special." As she says that last part, she looks at me sweetly and I instantly feel welcomed and at ease.

Holly and Gloria get called over to the door as another guest arrives, giving Ryan and I a moment alone.

"How you doing so far, Brooks? You feeling OK?" Ryan leans in and rubs his hands down my arms, intertwining his fingers with mine.

I nod reassuringly at him. "I like your family. They seem nice."

"Yeah, well the night is young." He sounds apologetic before looking sadly off into the distance.

"So, do I get the grand tour, or what?" I ask, trying to lighten the mood.

He snaps right back to playful Ryan. "Admit it, Brooks, you just want to see my old bedroom." He smirks at me suggestively.

"You caught me. Now let's see it."

Ryan takes my hand and leads me up the giant staircase. We walk a short way down the left hallway, stopping at a closed door all the way at the end. Ryan opens the door and nods for me to go inside. I take a look around, noticing the messy bookshelves, dresser drawers that have clothes peeking out, and assorted items strewn about—a skateboard, hockey stick, video game system, and assorted magazines and books. It's like he never left.

I think about how neat and meticulous his current apartment is and find it funny. "You'd think your mom could afford a housekeeper or something. You're pretty messy, Blake. Or at least you used to be . . ."

I walk around, trying to soak in little details, desperate to understand just a little bit more about this confusing, complicated man I'm growing to like more and more.

"Yeah, well when I was here I didn't give a shit about much. As soon as I was able to get out, I took the few things I needed and left the rest. I think my mom still has some twisted fantasy that I never really left." He keeps his hands in his pockets, arms stiff. Clearly being back in this room makes him uncomfortable.

Before I turn to leave I catch a glimpse of a photo sticking out from one of the stacks of books on the desk. I pull it out to reveal a little boy and a girl standing on a beach. The boy is tickling the girl, who has a giant, beaming smile on her face. The boy's blue eyes—that I'd recognize anywhere—are lit up with such obvious, pure joy I can't help but feel happy, too.

"You and Hazel?"

Ryan comes up behind me and takes the photo from my hand. A small smile forms on his lips. "Yeah. We used to go to Peyton Cove every summer. It was my favorite place. There's this huge beach that stretches out for miles and miles. When you stand out there it's just you, the waves, the sand, and the sky. Nothing else seems to matter." He scoffs and put the photo back on the desk. "It was nice when life was a lot less complicated, right?" Before I have a chance to respond, Ryan's pointing toward the hall. "We should really get back down before my mom comes looking for us. The more we can stay under Holly Blake's radar, the better."

Sensing he no longer wants to relive his past, I agree and

follow him out.

As we make our way back downstairs, we hear our names called across the adjacent dining room. Kinsley and Lucas are standing with Eli, Logan, and Tristan so we make our way over.

"Hey, man. How're you holding up?" Lucas slaps Ryan on the back. Ryan remains calm as he replies with a monotone, "Fan-fucking-tastic," before shaking hands with Eli.

Logan and Tristan acknowledge each of us before Tristan eyes me and blurts out, "I still can't fucking believe you two. Never in a million years would I peg you as a family man." He jostles Ryan, who looks pissed. "Oh come on, Blake. We all know your rules about keeping your shit quiet, but you can't deny the fact you basically invented the hit it and quit it game. This girl must have some pretty special moves to get you to stick around for more." Tristan wiggles his eyebrows, clearly alluding to Ryan's unchaste past.

While this isn't exactly news to me, something about being reminded about all the women Ryan's been with makes my stomach flip. Hopefully it's just the baby. Also, I don't know much about their relationship, but every time the four guys are together there definitely seems to be some unspoken tension between Ryan and Tristan.

As if aware of the brewing hostility, Tristan's twin brother, Logan, quickly breaks in. "I, for one, think it's about time this guy found a girl ballsy enough to handle him. Luc tells me you don't take any of his shit, which is the way it should be." Logan grins at me, his dimpled cheeks and blond hair making a lethally charming combination. Logan and Lucas are business partners, and from what I hear their venture capital firm is doing really well.

Kinsley steps in to say, "You're all just jealous." She slides over to hug me before pulling back to look at my stomach. "Ah you look beautiful, Kells. How are you feeling?"

"I'm really good. Sorry I've been so out of touch lately. Things have been crazy." I'm suddenly hit with just how much I've missed her.

As if she can tell how much I need to talk, she hooks her arm in mine and leads me away from the boys to a quieter corner.

"How are things with you and Ry? How's the baby?" Kinsley nudges me excitedly, anxious to hear all the details.

Do I really want to admit the most recent sexual development of my relationship with Ryan? I decide to focus on her second question. "The baby is good. Still growing and making me hungry as hell. Seriously, I feel like I could eat an entire cow."

She giggles, but doesn't let me off the hook. "And things with Ryan are good? Lucas told me what a big deal it is he let you inside his place, let alone move in, so it's got to be strange spending so much time together."

A puzzling look passes over my face. "What do you mean it's a big deal?"

Kinsley looks thrown. "He didn't tell you that you're the first girl he's ever had in his apartment? Hell, the first girl to even know where he lives, let alone get inside."

I think back to Darrin's reaction when I moved in, and how Ryan brushed off the comment as if it didn't mean anything. Why the hell wouldn't he tell me?

I don't want to dwell on it so I hide my disappointment. "Things are good. We're sort of friends now." I try to appear innocent, avoiding eye contact but can feel her staring. "What?"

She gives me a knowing look. "You know, Kells, that's the same look I used to get when it came to answering questions about Lucas."

I shrug. "OK, so we have sex sometimes, but we both know it's only practical while we stick with this whole fake engagement thing. I am fully aware it means nothing."

"It's kind of hard for it to mean nothing when you're carrying his baby, Kelley." Kinsley looks at me gently. "I just want to make sure you're all right. I know how you feel about true love and everything, so going through this has got to be tough."

Across the room I can see Ryan leaning back on a side table while Logan and Tristan talk animatedly. Man, why does he always have to be so damn good looking? I realize in this moment that yes, I do feel something when it comes to Ryan. I feel lucky that this smart, successful, loyal man is my friend. So what if we're not meant to have a real romantic relationship? I can be myself around him, and that's when you know you truly trust someone.

"It's not so bad. I'm glad we're helping each other through this. He really is a good guy, Kins. Even though he's not the one, he's a good friend and I know he'll be a great dad."

Kinsley nods her head. "Lucas says Ryan has been through some serious shit, but next to Luc he's the most loyal guy I know." She looks lovingly at her husband, who catches her eyeing him and smiles warmly. "But take it from me, Kell. Those are exactly the kinds of guys that make you realize you want something you never even considered."

I pause at Kinsley's words. The thing is I know what I want—I want true love and passion and a husband and a family. But I also know these are not things I will be able to have for a while, so I might as well make the best of things with Ryan while we ride out this fake engagement. My eyes are open and I know what this is, so there's no harm in being really good friends who are going to have a baby together. At least for now.

I decide I'm parched and excuse myself to the kitchen. I ask a waiter for a glass of water and he disappears into a back room. As I wait patiently for him to return, Gloria walks in. When she spots me she comes right over.

"There's that pretty girl who's going to be my new grand-daughter. I sure hope Ryan is behaving himself around you." She grins knowingly and I can't help but smile back.

"Well, I do have to put him in his place sometimes, but he takes care of me."

Gloria pats my arm. "He needs a strong-willed woman to put up with him. I'm glad he had the sense to scoop you up when he had the chance." She grabs my hands and examines the beautiful ring on my left hand. "And my ring looks like it was made for you." She gets a wistful look as my eyes snap up to hers.

"Your ring?" I ask, confused.

She nods and brushes her fingers across the band. "My Winston gave me this fifty-three years ago. Although he passed when Ryan was only eight, he was a good man and the love of my life. When Ryan was old enough I gave him this ring and told him to give it to someone extra special. I'm glad he listened." She looks at me with such genuine adoration I instantly feel guilty for being a complete and utter fraud.

I go numb and can barely speak. The surprising blows just keep on coming tonight. I manage to return her smile and nod, thankful the waiter interrupts us by handing me my water. Gloria gives my hand one last squeeze before making her way out of the room to talk with someone else.

Conflicting emotions play tug of war with my heart, going from feeling touched and honored to seething with anger. On the one hand it is very sweet he gave me such a meaningful family heirloom, but on the other it makes me extremely pissed off. He knows what we have is temporary and isn't real, so is this just some big fucking joke? Am I so inconsequential that he didn't think this would be a giant slap in the face? *Here, Brooks. Come live with me like it's no big deal and hey, why not wear this incredibly*

*meaningful ring for a few months while we pretend to be engaged? And
then I'll take it back and someday give it to the real girl I'm going to
spend my life with and we can all laugh about it.*

The room gets smaller as the walls close in and I look around
at all the strangers I don't know. They are all wearing such fancy
clothes and are talking and laughing and I feel very out of place.
My heart starts to race and it's hard to breathe. I could use some
air . . .

As my shitty luck would have it, before I can make it to the
door I'm stopped by none other than Holly Blake.

"Kelley, darling. Is everything all right? You look a bit pale."
She looks at me with pitying eyes and all I can do is stare back,
not sure what to say as I try to keep my anxiety in check. I'm
feeling confused enough about Ryan as it is without having to
deal with his family, too. She simply pats my arms and says in an
annoying, condescending tone, "It's all right, dear. I know this
can be a lot to take in." She looks proudly around the room. "I
always knew Ryan would turn out to be so successful. It must
be overwhelming for someone like you to see where he came
from, being that it's so extravagant. I did everything I could to
make sure he had every advantage in life, and look at him now.
He owns his own law firm, has a nice apartment, and now he's
starting a family with such a pretty young girl. It just makes me
so happy to know I did right by him."

She looks downright pleased with herself and I suddenly
want to scream. I don't miss her not-so-subtle dig about *"someone
like me,"* but that aside I think I'm more upset by her taking credit
for Ryan's success. As frustrated as I might be at him, I can't let
this awful woman say these things. I think back to the anguished
look on Ryan's face when he opened up about his family the other night, and that's all it takes for me to ball my hands into fists,
trying to hold back my unexpected anger. I know I should just

keep my mouth shut—just bite my tongue until it bleeds—but I can't. "I'm pretty sure Ryan got to where he is all on his own."

Holly glares daggers at me before her sweet smile returns. "Excuse me?"

I feel panicked for a second, knowing this isn't my place, but this vile woman patting herself on the back for how amazing Ryan is really ticks me off. He might come off as an arrogant ass sometimes, but he's *my* arrogant ass and I won't let anyone mess with him. Call it loyalty or call it crazy hormones, but I'm so worked up now I can't back down. "I mean he's had a hard life, no thanks to you, and it's because of his own dedication and hard work he's gotten to where he is."

This makes Holly stand straighter, as she clasps her hands in front of her, the fake, creepy smile still in place. Seriously, is it botoxed on her face or something? Her voice sounds both sweet and threatening when she speaks. "I'm sorry, but I really don't think this is any of your business."

Now I get really pissed. Part of me knows she is absolutely right, but I'm feeling upset and attacked so before I can stop the words, the lie tumbles out of my mouth harshly. "Considering I'm going to be his wife, I think it's plenty of my business."

Holly looks like I slapped her in the face. "Just because you were sneaky enough to trick my son into impregnating you does not mean you have a right to judge me." The icy tone of her words is enough to make me shiver.

That's it, the claws are coming out. "At least I know I'll be a better mother to our baby than you were to Ryan."

Fire dances in her eyes. Her voice remains calm and even, but by the way she grits her teeth I can tell she's trying really hard not to lose her shit in front of her guests. "How *dare* you say such terrible things about me in my own home when I was nice enough to invite you for this special day. I think you should leave."

Before I have time to respond, I hear a very pissed off Ryan yelling, "What the fuck? Did I seriously just hear you try to kick my fiancée out?"

CHAPTER

fifteen

Ryan

I STALK NEXT TO KELLEY, putting a reassuring hand on the small of her back before turning my rage back to my mother. As soon as I saw her get Kelley alone I knew shit would start, and it's a good thing I came over when I did.

These past few weeks have been good with Kelley and me. Real good. After I fucked her bare in the shower I just about lost my mind—I've never had sex without a condom, and not only was it the first time I screwed the same woman more than once, but it was the only time I ever wanted to. And that is dangerous territory. Thankfully I was able to get my shit together and realize we have to stay friends. That's all I'm capable of right now.

While I may not understand what the fuck I'm really feeling for this girl, I sure as shit know I will not let anybody hurt her, especially my fucked up family.

My mom glances around the room, smiling, making sure

we're not causing a scene. She leans in and tries to reason with me. "Ryan, darling, please don't be upset with me. I've been nothing but kind to your friend here and she has said such nasty things about me. Quite frankly you might want to reconsider your relationship. For her to say I had nothing to do with your upbringing is just appalling. I'm your mother for goodness sake."

I don't back down, nor do I lower my voice. "First of all, she's more than my friend, she's the fucking mother of my child, so you better start treating her with some respect. And secondly, I heard what she said, and it was the goddamned truth." If I thought I liked Kelley before, after hearing her stand up to my mother I downright worship her.

My mother looks horrified as she notices people can hear us. "Ryan, this is not the time nor the place for you to speak to me this way."

Words cannot describe the level of protectiveness I feel toward Kelley hearing my mother give her shit, and right now I don't care if the whole fucking house hears us. "What's the matter, mother? Are you afraid people will know the fucking truth for once?"

I can tell Kelley is uncomfortable next to me, but I refuse to let my mom get away with this. Not this time. I brought Kelley into this three-ring shit show, so if anything it's my mess to clean up. She did nothing wrong but try to stand up for me, and I'm sure as hell going to defend her.

"Ryan Bartholomew Blake, where is all this hostility coming from?"

I just laugh. "You've got to be fucking kidding me. How about from when you ignored Hazel and I after Dad walked out? How about from when you refused to notice your teenage son became an alcoholic? Or maybe it's from when you practically left your only daughter to die from some fucking drug overdose until I had to threaten you to help her?" I ball my fists, squeezing them tight at my sides. I've held onto this anger for a long time, and it's about time I finally let some of it out.

I don't think I've ever seen my mother look so completely stunned. She stands frozen and her fake smile finally fades. After a minute she clears her throat and collects herself enough to tersely state, "I'm sorry you feel that way," before briskly leaving the room and disappearing into the crowd.

I feel a hand on my shoulder and find Eli standing next to me. "Everything ok, son?"

I nod, still tensed, and he pats me on the back with understanding in his eyes. I turn my attention to Kelley, who looks like she might pass out. "Let me grab our coats and we'll get out of here." Lucas and Kinsley make their way over, knowing enough not to say anything. Luc and his dad know the kind of shit my mom usually pulls, which is why I'm grateful they still came to support me.

A few seconds later I'm helping Kelley into her jacket and ushering her out of the house to the safety of my truck. I turn the key so it roars to life and maneuver us down the drive. We sit in silence as I pull onto the main road.

"Brooks? Will you please say something?" I feel out of my element as I worry about both her and the baby. She looked white as a fucking ghost inside and I will never forgive myself if this causes her to break.

She remains quiet for a minute longer and I worry something is seriously wrong. But then I hear her sweet, light voice cut through the awkward thickness. "Your middle name is Bartholomew?"

Fuck, this girl is going to be the death of me.

We both chuckle before she gets serious. "I'm really sorry for what happened in there, Ry. I didn't mean to make things worse between you and your mom."

Her voice is unexpectedly quiet and sad. She's usually so bold and feisty, so this makes my heart fucking shatter. She never needs to apologize for speaking the truth. "I promise there is nothing you could say that would make things worse between my mother and I. This shit was a long time coming, and I am fucking thankful you stood up to her. It's about damn time somebody did."

"Yeah, well the whole evening was pretty unfuckingbelievable." She sounds pissed now, and I don't blame her.

I feel shitty for bringing her into my mess. I'm not sure how to make it up to her so I stay quiet, hoping we can just forget the whole fucking thing.

By the way she tenses and stares out the window, I don't think that's likely.

WE SPEND THE REST OF the drive in complete silence. When I finally pull the truck into the parking garage I let my eyes shift over to Kelley, trying to gauge how she's feeling. It's clear she has a lot on her mind and has been stewing about it the whole way home. "Talk to me, Brooks."

She shifts in her seat and holds up her left hand. "Why did you give me this ring?"

Expecting her to rant about how horrible my mother is, I'm surprised this is the direction she's going in. "Because we agreed to pretend we're engaged?" I ask, legitimately confused.

She looks me square in the eye as she clarifies. "Why the hell did you give me your *grandmother's* ring?"

I rub my hand down my face. *Fuck.* "I guess you talked to Grams then?"

Before I have a chance to explain, she's crossing her arms

and eyeing me accusingly. "And why didn't you tell me you've never let any other girl into your apartment? Is our relationship so completely meaningless and fake that it doesn't even occur to you to mention the simplest of things?"

Her eyes fill with so much hurt that I feel completely in the dark. Where the fuck is all this coming from? I try to remain calm. "What the hell are you talking about?"

She shakes her head and rolls her eyes before un-clicking her seatbelt and opening the door. As she gets out she spits, "You, Ryan Blake, are an asshole." And then she slams the door and stalks toward the apartment building.

I quickly hop out of my seat to follow. Half of me is pissed, and half of me is worried her anger is bad for the baby. For a pregnant chick she sure moves fast, and by the time I get into the lobby the elevator doors are dinging closed. I try to keep my shit together as I mash the button and wait for it to come back down. I hear Darrin from across the hall.

"Shit, Ryan. What happened? That girl was one mad firecracker tonight."

I hang my head and lean against the wall, exhausted from everything that's happened. "I wish I knew, D. This is why relationships suck. Sure the sex is fun in the beginning, but you just get fucked in the end."

Darrin laughs in his signature deep, hearty way. "Yeah, it's no secret all women will drive you mad at some point. But I tell ya, Ry, some women—like that girl up there,"—he points to the ceiling—"... well sometimes they are worth every single ounce of trouble." I scoff before Darrin continues. "As a proud father of five and seasoned husband of thirty years, can I offer you a piece of advice?"

I shrug. "It's worth a shot."

"When your lady is pissed like that, it's usually about

something she's going through rather than anything you did. You're just the easiest target, so do both of yourselves a favor and take the fucking bullet."

The elevator door slides open and he nods at me before going back to looking at some paperwork on the desk beside him. I sigh and get in, pushing the button for floor E. I open the unlocked apartment door slowly, afraid Kelley might start tossing shit. I've never seen her so angry before, and I wouldn't be surprised if she's a thrower. But everything is dark and quiet so I take off my jacket and make my way to the bedroom, ready to take Darrin's advice and eat lead.

Kelley is curled up on her side, facing away from me. I lean against the doorjamb, not liking how I feel seeing her look so small and fragile. I try to keep my voice calm and soft. "Brooks, can you please tell me what the hell is going on?"

When she doesn't answer right away I move closer and sit on the side of the bed. I rub her shoulder, which is when I hear her sniffling. Shit. Now I'm determined to make her smile. "Come on, you usually don't have any trouble telling me what you're thinking."

I give her a playful nudge, and she sniffles louder before rolling over. Her face is red and splotchy, with wet streaks smudging the mascara under her eyes. I still think she looks beautiful, and I have to resist the urge to kiss her pouty, swollen lips.

"I'm sorry for getting so upset. Blame your kid in here for making my emotions go crazy."

I reach out and rub her stomach. "I forgive the little tike." I smile, fucking relieved she's not going to yell again.

"And I'm sorry I called you an asshole. Even if it is a little true." She sniffles and I laugh. She lets out a big sigh before explaining. "I just think our situation has gotten too complicated. I mean there you were, yelling at your mother in the middle of a party all because of me. Because I couldn't keep my big mouth shut."

I cut in. "I already told you, you have nothing to be sorry for. My mother was the one who was wrong."

Kelley throws her head back and stares at the ceiling. "But that's just it, Ry. She wasn't wrong. I'm not really your fiancée so it really isn't any business of mine what goes on in your family. In six months it's not even going to matter, so you had to defend me for nothing."

Is that what this is all about? She thinks I don't actually care about her? That I only stood up for her because of our lie? "Fuck, Brooks, is that really what you think? That as soon as this baby comes I'll kick you out on your ass and we'll pretend to barely know each other?" I stand up, getting agitated. Doesn't she see I'm trying here?

"I'm just saying this is harder for me than I thought it would be. Trust me, I still completely understand the deal we made and I don't want to change it," She swings her legs to dangle off the bed, but stays sitting on the edge. "I just didn't realize how comfortable I would get being around you. It's sort of how I always pictured my life, but it's twisted and backwards. When I was actually engaged to Jake I felt like we were strangers. We barely spent time together and he never did anything remotely protective. He didn't even want our baby, actually wanted me to get rid of it. And now I'm pregnant with your child after what was supposed to be one stupid night, we live together and sleep in the same bed and have sex, but our relationship is a complete joke." She lets out a sad chuckle. "I can't ever seem to get it right."

That makes me stop dead in my tracks and stare at her. "It has never been a fucking joke to me, Kelley." She flinches at my words and I realize they came out louder than I meant them to. I'm pissed at her for thinking I don't take this seriously, and pissed at her fucking ex for treating her like shit. What kind of sick fuck tells his girl to abort their baby? Darrin's advice echoes in my mind as I recall everything Kelley told me at the wedding in regards to how she views relationships and love, which makes me soften my voice and kneel in front of her. "Look, I know that what we're doing doesn't make any fucking sense, but you have to believe that I have never said or done anything with you that I regret. I want to have this kid with you and I asked you to move in here and I gave you my grandmother's ring all because I wanted to. Even if we both know there's no way in hell I'm Prince Fucking Charming, I care about you and you will always be special to me. I realize now it wasn't fair of me to drag you into all of this because of my own fucked up past and insecure shit. You deserve to be happy with someone you actually like, Brooks. I mean that."

She looks down at her lap and blushes. "I do like you, Ryan. You're my best friend."

Fuck. I am an asshole for being too selfish to admit she deserves better than this. Better than me. She's the type of girl who needs passion and romance, and I am just not that fucking guy. For the first time in my whole entire life I wish I was—for her sake—but I'm just not. Ever since I turned my life around after it turned to shit when I was a teenager, I've purposely kept my distance from women. I couldn't even be there for my sister when she needed me most, let alone try and start something with someone who isn't my own flesh and blood. Love is not something I'm capable of and I don't know how to date or any of that other sweet guy bullshit, but I know I can try to do whatever it takes to make sure this beautiful, feisty girl in front of me is always safe. "And you're mine, Brooks, so if you want out of this just say the word. I'll still help you and the baby in any way I can, but if pretending to be together is too much just say the fucking word and I'll take care of it. And I'll make sure everyone knows it's my fault."

She looks into my eyes and I see so many conflicting emotions staring back at me it's hard to tell which one is winning out. In a quiet yet firm voice she responds, "That's not what I want, Blake. This is my fault as much as it is yours and we're in so deep now, we might as well finish it. I just get anxious not knowing what's going to happen or how this will all play out. I'm so afraid of what people will think of me if they find out the truth . . ."

I move to sit next to her on the bed, putting my arm around her shoulders. *Damn, she's always so soft and warm.* "Well, since we like each other, and you're stuck with my sorry ass for at least another six months, how about we agree to take it a day at a time and worry about the future when we get there? Let's just enjoy each other and fuck what anybody else thinks, OK?"

I pull her close and can feel her smile into my chest as she says in a muffled voice, "Ok, sounds like a plan, Bartholomew."

Shit, this girl knows how to get me every time. My turn. "Besides, you know you can't get enough of my hot body." I lift my eyebrows seductively. "One taste had you coming back for more."

This makes her laugh out loud, so I know we're good. At least for now.

Still holding her close, I lay us both back on the pillows so she's half draped on top of me. I'm so comfortable I'm about to fall asleep when I hear Kelley's tired voice pull me back awake.

"Ry?"

"Yeah, babe?"

"I'm sorry you have to lie to your mom. I know you hate how fake she is, but I want you to know you're nothing like her."

My chest feels like it's in a vise hearing her say nice shit like that to me. I don't deserve how good and kind she is, especially after tonight. "I sure hope you're fucking right on that one, Brooks."

"I really liked your sister and your Grams, though. They make me feel just as safe as you do. I'm sorry we have to lie to them."

"I'm glad you got to meet them. They can see how much I care about you, and that's no lie." It's the honest fucking truth.

She wraps her arm tighter around my waist, snuggling her face in my chest. I rub small circles down her back, which makes her entire body soften. Just when I think she's fallen asleep, she says in a sleepy voice, "You're going to be a really good dad, Blake. I want you to know that, too."

Unable to form words due to the sudden tightness in my throat, I move my lips to press a soft kiss to the top of her head as my reply. We both give in to sleep, and my last thought before I lose consciousness is that for a guy who never cuddles, I sure as shit could get used to this.

CHAPTER

sixteen

Twenty Weeks

Kelley

"CONGRATULATIONS MOM AND DAD . . . IT'S a boy!"

Dr. Conners beams as she moves the ultrasound wand over my stomach. Ryan starts fist pumping, and I groan. "Oh great, just what the world needs, another Blake boy." I roll my eyes, trying to conceal a smile as I tease, but for once it does nothing to change the huge grin plastered across his face. I'm glad for that.

He looks damn smug as he replies. "Fuck yeah it does." He moves to get a closer look at the small screen, tilting his head left, then right, before pointing to one of the black and white shapes. "And looks like he already takes after me. Is that his—?."

Dr. Conners laughs as I swat Ryan's arm. He gives me a not-so-innocent '*What?*' look. "Sorry to disappoint, Ryan, but that's just his leg." Dr. Conners proceeds to point out all of the anatomical parts of our child, much to Ryan's fascination.

"I'm going to teach this kid so much cool shit." He looks at me excitedly before kissing me on the forehead, a gesture I'm beginning to love. After our talk a month ago we've put a lot less pressure on defining our relationship, and things have been really good since then. Just like Ryan said, we're taking things one day at a time, and I feel happier than I have in a long time. I'm not worried about the future or how my life is supposed to turn out, I'm just enjoying being here, knowing that our son is healthy. Our *son*. I'll admit a part of me had hoped I would get to buy all sorts of cute dresses and bows for a sweet baby girl, but the more I see Ryan's genuine smile and bright eyes, I can't help but feel more than proud to have a little boy that looks just like him. And god help all the mothers who do have little girls, because I just know he'll be devilishly handsome and infuriatingly charming, just like his dad.

A WEEK LATER I'M SITTING at work going over some new commercial listings when a knock at my office door startles me. Gemma is standing in the doorway, holding an awkwardly large package.

"This was just delivered for you." Her small arms struggle to hold the box as I rush over to help place it on my desk.

"Thanks, Gemma. Do you know who it's from?" I scan the box for any indication, wondering what it could be.

Gemma shakes her head. "No idea, but from the size of it I'm sure it's gotta be something really great."

She smiles before exiting my office, leaving me alone to find out what's inside. I tear off the brown paper to reveal a white box wrapped with a silver silk bow. I pull the ribbon and open the top, shoving aside the piles of ivory colored tissue paper to reveal a thick, plum colored coat and matching knit hat. A simple white card is folded on top.

Sunshine -
When you get home tonight put these on and be ready by six.
Don't argue, just do it.
x R
P.S. The coat & hat are for you, but the rest is for me ;)

My heart swells as I pull the hat over my head and reach for the pretty jacket. I pull it out of the box to get a better look, which reveals a black lace bra and matching panties tucked underneath. I chuckle, realizing the meaning of Ryan's note. The guy is good, I'll give him that. This surprise is so unexpected and so unlike Ryan that I find myself feeling giddy at the possibility of what he has in store for us tonight. I pile everything into the box, and try to focus back on my work, but am too excited to concentrate.

At five o'clock I rush home, box in tow, and wait for Ryan to arrive.

At quarter to six I hear the elevator ding from the hall and hold my breath as Ryan walks through the door. He smiles when he sees me standing in the living room, wearing the coat and hat. "I see you got my present." He eyes me from head to toe appreciatively.

I revel in his stare, letting him take it all in. "Yup. I got the box and your note and did exactly what you said." I smile sweetly, and he immediately knows something is up.

He puts his things down on the kitchen counter before making his way over to me. "It can't be that easy, Brooks. It's never that easy with you." He smirks, knowing me too well.

I keep my composure and shrug innocently. "I came home, put on what was in the box, and am here waiting for you. Just like the note said." He moves to stand in front of me, and I untie the coat's belt, pulling it open to reveal me in nothing but the lace bra and panties underneath. "See, I can follow directions quite well."

I smile seductively as Ryan's eyes turn a shade darker. His hunger is obvious. He moves his hands to my hips, getting as close as he can with my growing stomach nestled between us. I can already feel how hard he is against my abdomen. "Fuck, Brooks. I'm going to have to tell you what to do more often."

His lips move down my neck, causing me to whimper. "You can try, but I can't promise I'll always be so willing to listen."

His mouth makes its way to my ear. "I'm sure you could be persuaded."

As his hands move to cup my lace covered ass, my knees buckle. "I don't know, Blake. You might have to ask real nice."

"Hey Brooks?" he mumbles into my neck.

"Mmmyeah?" My voice is raw and breathless.

"Stop talking." His mouth crashes fiercely down on mine, silencing me anyway.

Normally I'd want to put up more of a fight, but hell, I'll do just about anything he says if it means his hands and mouth will continue to raid my body. His right hand moves to cup the back of my neck while his left simultaneously slides down in between my legs. I gasp as soon as I feel his palm rub against my most sensitive part. I grip his shoulders for support as he wastes no time stretching me with two broad fingers.

Breaking our kiss, Ryan's lust-filled gaze locks onto mine. "We have to make this quick so I need you to come for me."

Not that I could form a coherent thought if I tried, but before I even have a chance to answer his lips are back on mine and his hand moves faster. He tightens his hold on me, and his commanding authority only makes this hotter. I sway my hips into his touch, unable to get enough. The pressure from his hand and the friction of the lace combined with his delicious tongue tangling with mine are enough to make me come apart. I cry out as my entire body goes numb with pleasure before letting my full weight fall in Ryan's arms.

He holds me steady, his right hand at my neck, his left still inside me. I lean into him for support, sighing in satisfaction.

"Come on, Brooks. We don't want to be late for your surprise."

When he slowly glides his hand out of me, I pout in protest. "You mean that wasn't it?" I ask breathlessly, which makes him chuckle into my hair.

"Babe, I'd gladly stay here and make you moan my name all night long, but then you'll never get to see where I plan to take you."

He grins, which has my muscles contracting again already, but I relent. I really do want to know where we're going. "Fine. Just let me put some clothes on."

I try to make my way to the bedroom, but he holds onto my hand. He frowns, looking conflicted as he takes another peek under my coat. "Fuck the surprise. We'll stay here."

He moves his hands back toward my chest, but I push him away, finally able to control myself. "Nice try, pal. It's not every day a woman gets taken out by *the* Ryan Blake. This is an opportunity I don't want to miss."

I try to pull away just as his phone starts to ring. He pulls it out and looks at the caller id before holding it up. "You're lucky you're saved by the bell. Be sure to dress warm and casual." He grins before giving my ass a light slap while simultaneously picking up the call. "Hey Luc, What's up?"

I shake my head and try to hide a smile as I head down the hall to get dressed. I throw on a pair of fleece-lined black leggings and a cream colored knit sweater under my coat. I leave the underwear on, hopeful when we get back I can experience a repeat performance of what just happened in the living room. My legs squeeze together in anticipation. I look at my reflection in the full size closet mirror and run my hand over my stomach. The coat fits comfortably, but is snug enough to really accentuate my rounded midsection. It doesn't bother me anymore that I seem to grow by the second. I feel like I can finally let go of my anxieties and enjoy the excitement of being pregnant. It might not be exactly how I pictured it happening, but I'm finally going to be a mom. I smile, thinking about Ryan's enthusiasm over having a son, which reminds me he is probably waiting so we can leave. I head back to the living room, but Ryan's raised voice makes me freeze before turning the corner at the end of the hall.

"I don't give a fuck what she says. I don't need her money or the fucking strings that come with it." There's a pause while I assume Lucas is talking before Ryan continues, "Yeah well she's fucking nuts if she thinks for one second I'm going to turn my back on Kelley or my son. Hell, they're more like my family than she is at this point, fake engagement and all."

I can't help but feel a warmth in my chest hearing him think of me as family. I tried not to think of our situation in those terms . . . it felt too weird. I guess I've been afraid it would make me feel even worse when it all ends, but maybe there's hope we can always hold onto a piece of it. Ryan's right—regardless of our relationship status, this baby will forever keep us connected in some way, and that thought actually reassures me.

I continue walking the rest of the way into the living room just as Ryan is hanging up. When he notices me, he smiles, not letting on that he just sounded agitated while taking on the phone. "Ready?"

I nod enthusiastically as he puts his hand on the small of my back and leads me to the door.

CHAPTER

seventeen

Ryan

"ARE WE THERE YET?"

"No."

"How about now?"

"Brooks . . ."

Kelley sits in the passenger seat of my truck and giggles at my warning tone, fully aware she's annoying the shit out of me. But fuck, I still find it cute as hell she's so excited. I just hope she likes where I'm taking her. Doing nice, surprising crap is not my style, but I figure if Kelley is going to put up with me it's the least I can do to try and make her feel special.

A few minutes later I pull into the entrance of Anderson Park, a big outdoor recreation area a few towns over. As I stop the truck and roll down my window at the ticket booth, Kelley looks at the sign plastered on the side of the small building that has "Date Night Drive-In" printed prominently across the top with tonight's feature displayed beneath.

"Oh my god, we're going to see *The Princess Bride*?" Kelley practically squeals and wiggles in her seat animatedly. I grin at her enthusiasm and pay the man at the booth. He tells me what radio station to tune into for the audio before directing me where to park. I pull my truck into an empty space in the open field, right in front of the large, white screen, and cut the ignition. When I look over to Kelley she looks like she's about ready to piss her pants. Or cry. Given her pregnant situation, both are likely.

"Ooh look! They have hot chocolate and cider doughnuts! Can we get some? Please can we?" Kelley pleads before practically hurling herself out of the truck. I follow suit and have to quicken my pace to keep up with her.

"Everything looks so magical. Like a winter wonderland." When we reach the short line at the pavilion serving snacks and drinks a few yards away she finally slows down. Pausing to look out at the entire park, illuminated by lamps and string lights, filling with people, she wraps her arms around her shoulders while crinkling her nose. "Seriously, Ryan. This is the best surprise. Thank you." She turns to me and her expression has my chest doing all sorts of weird shit.

I casually shrug. "Don't mention it." Our turn is up at the counter and I order two hot chocolates and two doughnuts. We have about a half hour to kill before the movie starts so when I see a small, unoccupied bench off to the left of the pavilion, I motion for us to sit. We eat our food and watch a group of kids playing in the light coating of snow that covers the ground. Even though we're bundled in warm coats—and Kelley has on her new hat—it's still cold as fuck so we huddle closer together for warmth.

Kelley's light voice finally breaks through our silence. "Can I tell you a secret?"

I finish my last bite of doughnut and ball up my napkin. "Shoot."

"I've never been to a drive-in before."

"Never?"

She shakes her head. "I didn't know they have them in the winter either. I thought it was just a summer thing."

"Lucky a client happened to tell me about this one then." All right, I *may* have asked for a little advice on where to take a girl, but she doesn't need to know that and think I'm a complete pussy who doesn't know the first thing about where to take a woman on a date. Even though I am, and I don't.

As if reading my mind, the next words out of Kelley's pretty, point-blank mouth are, "Is this a date?"

Fuck. Is it?

"I guess normal engaged people date, right?" I reply casually.

She laughs out loud. "Blake, we are *so* not normal people."

I grunt in amusement. "Ain't that the fucking truth."

Amidst her dying laughter I feel Kelley shiver. I instinctively put my arm around her shoulders, pulling her close to my chest.

She grabs onto my waist, snuggling closer. "This is nice."

Even though it's about thirty degrees out, I feel my temperature rise having Kelley pressed against me. It's actually really fucking nice being with her, so I easily agree, "Yeah, it is."

She tilts her head up to me. Something about the way her eyes darken and her mouth parts has me wanting to fuck the hell out of her right here even if small children are present. I'm about to say screw it and do just that when I hear a male voice.

"Kelley?"

I don't miss the hint of frustration that flashes in her eyes at our interruption before she focuses on the guy standing in front of us. His jet black hair is slicked back and he's wearing an expensive looking long, black coat with leather gloves. I can immediately sense he's a douche. I mean who the fuck wears goddamn loafers to a drive-in movie when it's fucking winter? Standing next to him is an average looking woman with short, blond hair pushing a baby stroller. I wouldn't even know there was a kid in there, buried with all the fucking blankets, if not for hearing a few muffled, cooing sounds.

"Jake?" Kelley whispers in disbelief. I can hear the surprise in her voice. I quickly recall all the shit she told me about this loser.

I stand up, pulling Kelley with me. I extend my hand forcefully, drawing Jake's attention. "Hey, man. Ryan Blake. You know my girl here?" I give her a possessive squeeze, claiming her. The asshat looks distrustfully at me before looking at Kelley to confirm.

She finally clears her throat. "Yeah, um, Ryan, this is Jake. Jake, this is Ryan."

"Her fiancé." I add, maybe a little too proudly.

Jake, seemingly unaffected, nods before turning to the woman subtly moving closer to him. "This is Carmen, my wife. Car, this is Kelley, an old friend. And this little guy is our son, Michael." He motions to the stroller before doing the same to Kelley's stomach. "I don't want to be presumptuous, but looks like you're expecting your own?" When Kelley nods he adds in a douchey, enthusiastic, "Congratulations."

I can feel Kelley tense beside me as she manages to reply, "Yeah, thanks. You too." The cocky bastard doesn't even seem to realize how uncomfortable this is—he just stands there smiling like a tool.

"I tell ya, you never know how much you can love someone until you have a kid. I'm just lucky I found this lady to bless me with such a gift." He puts his arm around his wife—who, I notice, stiffens at his touch—and he looks blissfully at their stroller.

It takes everything in me not to punch this dickhole in the fucking throat. Not only does he have the balls to talk about Kelley as if they barely knew each other, but then he flaunts his family right in front of her? As if the shit they went through wouldn't have any affect on her. Fuck this.

I'm about to let loose on him when the giant projection screen lights up and people begin hurrying back to their cars. I feel Kelley squeeze my hand and her sad fucking eyes silently plead with me to let it go. The prick is lucky as fuck. I simply offer a curt, "We better get going," before getting us as far the fuck away from them as possible.

I lead Kelley to the passenger side of my truck but pin her back against it before opening the door, caging her in.

"Talk to me, Brooks."

She lets out a sigh. "That was just fucking weird. I'm sorry we ran into him." She keeps her eyes down so I put my right hand under her chin, forcing her to look at me.

"I'm not. In fact I'm fucking glad we did." She stares at me, confused. "Now I know firsthand what an asshole he is and can sleep like a friggin' baby tonight knowing you didn't give birth to his evil spawn." That makes the smallest hint of a smile slip past her lips, but her eyes remain hurt. It guts me up that some jackass she should just forget about put it there. "I might have my own stupid shit going on, but I would never treat you like he just did. Ever, Brooks, do you hear me?"

She nods under my sincere stare, but sticks out her bottom lip in a sad pout. I want to kiss it—kiss all her pain away—but don't. Yeah, as if life was that fucking simple.

"Come on," I reach behind her to pull open the passenger door. I quickly adjust the seat so it's pushed all the way back and reach over to put my keys in the ignition, starting the radio. Then I climb in, pulling Kelley to sit between my legs. It's a little cramped so I have to wrap my arms around her midsection. She lays her head back on my chest as the lights go out and the movie's opening scene flashes on the screen. I feel her relax into my arms as we get sucked into a world of pirates, princesses, and true love.

It's entertaining enough, but what a bunch of garbage.

CHAPTER

eighteen

Twenty-four Weeks

Kelley

"CRAP."

I slam my phone down on the kitchen counter and mutter a few more choice curse words, startling Ryan who looks at me questioningly.

"My parents are coming."

He looks like he's ready to burst out laughing, but my death stare has him keeping his shit together. He smartly opts to try and comfort me. "You met my mother, remember? Nothing could be worse than that experience."

I lean on the stool next to him, facing the opposite direction. He instinctively rubs small circles on my lower back. "You don't get it, Ry. Your mom might be a bitch, but my parents are nice.

Like, *too* nice. It's awful."

"Wow, nice parents. Yeah, I can see how that must be fucking terrible."

Sarcastic bastard. "It is!" I glare at him over my shoulder before dropping my head. I want to be mad at him for making fun of me but his hands are massaging all the right spots on my aching back. I have to stifle a moan. I swivel around to face him, needing to focus on how best to explain Lila and Hal Brooks.

"You know how your mom ignored you growing up?" He nods, his jaw tensing like it always does at the mention of his mother. "My parents were the polar opposite. They believed in 'hands on' parenting and got super involved in every aspect of my life. That was fine when I was three, but as I got older it was terrible. They're so disgustingly open sometimes it's embarrassing."

He still doesn't look convinced that this is a problem, so I know I have to give him an example. "When I was in third grade I had a friend over and my mom started asking us about which boys in class we thought were cute, which turned into a mortifying hour long conversation about sex, complete with a visual demonstration using some of my dolls. My dad overheard and they started debating which positions were best 'for her pleasure.' We were fucking eight years old, Ryan!" I shudder at the memory. Needless to say that friend was never allowed back at my house after that. No wonder I moved two hours away from them . . .

Ryan looks like he's about to burst. "Is that why you waited so long to give it up?" He attempts to contain his laughter, but can't.

I lightly shove his arm. "Ha. Ha. Very funny." I knew I'd regret telling him the truth about my pathetic sex life.

I get up to leave but he grabs my arm. "Come on, Brooks. You have to admit it's pretty ironic. I grew up without any sort of openness or affection and turned into a man-whore while you were smothered with it and basically strapped on a fucking chastity belt." He tries to catch his breath in between chuckles.

"Yeah, fucking hilarious," I reply dryly. I fail to see why my childhood humiliation is so entertaining to him.

I stalk to the bedroom and hear him call out, "Hey, maybe they can give us a few pointers when they visit." That makes him laugh even harder.

Ok, maybe that's a little funny. But I refuse to let him know that, so I respond by calling out, "I hate you," before collapsing onto the bed with my arm draped over my face.

THE NEXT WEEK I'M PACING around the apartment like some type of madwoman. My parents are due to arrive any minute. I haven't seen them in eight months and I'm dreading what might happen when they meet Ryan. They know about the baby and the engagement, but I didn't go into much detail. I feel bad for not always returning my mother's phone calls, but she asks too many questions. Questions I'm not ready to answer.

Ryan is sitting on the couch, flipping through channels on the tv. "Brooks, if you don't sit still you're going to wiggle that kid right out of you."

"Good. At least if I go into labor we'll get out of doing this today. Might be the perfect plan." I pace faster.

"Yeah, and I'm sure only letting the baby cook for six months is a great plan, too." He grunts.

"Shut up." I don't need his sarcasm right now. I'm too busy thinking of an exit strategy.

I love my parents, I really do. And I know I'm lucky they care so much, especially after meeting Ryan's monster of a mother. But they know me better than anyone and I'm afraid they will take one look at Ryan and me together and know it's all a complete sham. They've only seen me with one man in my life—the man I thought was going to make all of my dreams come true but turned into a nightmare instead—and I really don't want to disappoint them again. They've only ever wanted me to be happy, and as much as I want that for myself, I want it so they can stop worrying about me, too. Neither of my parents have any boundaries, and I can see our web of lies quickly unraveling with their prying. The worst part? I can totally see Ryan and them getting along.

A knock has me stopping dead in my tracks. When I make no move to answer it, Ryan clicks off the tv and chuckles as he makes his way past me to open the door himself.

My mother immediately wraps Ryan in a huge hug and kisses his cheeks, her red lips—that accent her medium length reddish-brown hair—leave behind a clear mark. It's almost comical to see her short, petite stature overpowering his tall, muscular one. "You must be my handsome soon-to-be son-in-law." She holds onto his shoulders and studies him before looking to me. "He's just as hot as you said he was."

Ryan gets a big shit-eating grin before my father squeezes his way in, grumbling "My turn, let me at him." My dad, about the same build and only a few inches shorter, reaches to shake Ryan's hand, simultaneously clapping him on the back. "Hey, son. So you're the one that knocked up my little princess, eh. Well good to meet ya. How they hangin'?"

I have to resist a literal face-palm.

My mother comes over to me and looks like she's about to cry when she pats my growing stomach. "Oh sweetie, I am so happy for you." She leans in for a hug, smelling of the same Jean Nate perfume she always wears. "Your breasts are huge. Hal, aren't they huge. Are they tender? You should try a heating pad or a warm bath." I blush at her unfiltered, albeit sweet, concern over my boobs.

I hug my dad next, smiling when he gently taps the tip of my nose, just like he's done my entire life. His short, salt and pepper hair looks a little lighter than I remember seeing last, but his gray eyes and round, red cheeks are the exact same—warm and welcoming. "Hey, kid. Where's the bathroom? I've gotta piss like a racehorse." I try not to wince as I point to the door down the hall.

It's only been two seconds and, true to form, they're already embarrassing the crap out of me.

As my mother makes herself right at home and heads to the living room, I catch Ryan looking at me with amusement.

"What?" I cringe, feeling self-conscious as to how crazy he must think my parents are . . . and me by association.

Thankfully he laughs as he drapes his arm around me and leads us to the couch. "I like them. Now I see where you get your bluntness from." A playful spark lights up his eyes, making me feel a tiny bit of relief.

After my father returns from the bathroom we all sit on the couch and catch up.

My mother wastes no time turning to Ryan. "So, tell me . . . what exactly is wrong with you?"

Ryan looks completely caught off guard. "Wrong with me?"

"Are you married?"

Ryan looks uncertainly at me as sweat forms on his brow. "Huh?"

"Do you have any weird fetishes? Are you a drug addict? A criminal? Secretly gay?"

I've never seen Ryan look so completely baffled and nervous. "No . . . Wait, what? No!"

My mom laughs lightly and slaps him playfully on the knee.

"Aww calm down, sweetie. I'm just trying to figure out why on earth my daughter felt the need to keep you such a secret for so long. She never mentioned you and then all of a sudden, wham!, you're engaged and having a baby." She holds her hands up in front of her, palms facing out. "I'm not judging, just curious."

Ryan visibly relaxes while I cut in. "Mom, I told you. We knew each other for a while, as friends, and then things between us just grew pretty fast."

I smile at Ryan, trying to convey a silent apology for this entire thing. He smiles back sympathetically before jumping in. "Yeah, Mrs. Brooks. I'm afraid a lot of that's my fault. After getting to know Kelley better I just looked at her one day and knew she was something special. It took me some time to get up the courage to let her know, and hell, sometimes I still don't think I do a good enough job of that. I wasted too much time not showing her how much she means to me, so once we decided to give things a shot, I've been selfish in keeping her all to myself."

I know he's just saying all of this to keep up with our story, but his eyes never leave mine as he says it, causing my heart to beat faster.

My mom's sniffling breaks our trance. "Oh well if that isn't just the sweetest thing I've ever heard. Hal, did you hear that?"

"There she goes with the waterworks . . . that's how you know you've won her over." My dad chuckles before focusing on Ryan, shrugging easily. "As long as you make my little girl happy, you're ok in my book, too. "

My mom takes a deep breath. "All right, enough of this mushy stuff. Tell me, how's my grandson doing? What about any wedding plans?" She looks excitedly between us.

"He's good, mom. The doctor says he's healthy and everything is on schedule." I rub my stomach, leaning back into the couch. "And we haven't talked much about the wedding. We'll deal with that sometime after he's born." I chew my lip, hoping I come off sounding nonchalant rather than nervous.

My dad leans toward Ryan. "If you want my opinion, all of that wedding hoopla nonsense is a big load of crap." Ryan and I both look to him, unsure where he's going with this. "What? If you love someone and want to marry her, you should just do it. No need to waste all your time and money planning a celebration for other people. Wedding favors? What a bunch of bullshit. Why do I need to give *you* a gift for coming to celebrate *me* and the love of my life?" He shakes his head. "Nah, just elope and let it be about the two of you—the only people who matter. And I'm not just saying that since I'm supposed to foot the bill." He winks and nudges Ryan with his elbow.

Ryan laughs. "I couldn't agree more."

My dad looks amused and impressed. "I knew I liked you."

I chuckle nervously. I always pictured having a big, fairytale wedding, but since there will never be any wedding, big *or* small, it's not worth arguing. I prefer the whole topic be dropped.

Thankfully my dad changes the subject and the rest of the afternoon is spent talking about anything but our pretend nuptials. We talk about my mom's book club, my dad's job as a grocery store manger, and what my aunts and uncles have been up to. Apparently *everybody* asks about me. My mom and I make dinner, and she helps me with the dishes as Ryan and my dad bond over some sports channel.

"You know, sweetie, I like this one." My mom nods toward Ryan, who is shouting at the tv with my dad. I finish washing a dish in the sink and hand it to my mom to dry.

I look over to Ryan, who looks completely content to be sitting back watching a game with his theoretical father-in-law. He yells something at the screen, and smiles when my dad calls the ref a hack. "Yeah, he's not so bad." I laugh lightly.

"He'll be a great husband and a great father. I can see that already. He's so much better for you than Jake ever was." This is news to me . . . I always thought my mom was sad after Jake and I broke up. I also think back to seeing Jake at the drive-in . . . how I felt nothing for him and how Ryan stood up for me.

"I thought you liked Jake?"

My mom clicks her tongue in disapproval. "I pretended to like him, for your sake, but I always thought he was bad news. You needed to make that mistake for yourself, but I was relieved when it ended. I love you sweetie, but you've always been too much of a romantic, and it broke my heart to see you blinded by that. Up until the end you looked at that boy like the sun rose and set with him and he let you do it, only to break your heart. No, Ryan's different. I can see what you guys have is different. You're perfect for each other."

Tears form in my eyes and I have the urge to spill everything about the truth. My mom would understand, right? But then I think of Ryan and our deal, and I settle for only admitting one small truth.

"We're far from perfect, mom. When it's good, it's really good. I actually believe we can make it and everything will be fine. But sometimes I get scared and think I'm making it all up. What if it's not real, just like last time?" I drop my head, trying to hold back the tears when I feel my mom come up behind me and squeeze my shoulders.

"Honey, it might not be perfect, but it's real. In fact, that's how you can tell." She kisses my cheek and goes back to drying the dishes, humming happily.

Real? How can something that's based on a lie ever be real?

CHAPTER

nineteen

Twenty-six Weeks

Ryan

IF I THOUGHT I WAS having a hard time keeping my emotions in check before, after meeting Kelley's parents I know I'm fucking boned. Figures that a cool-as-fuck girl like her would have two fucking cool parents. I know she's embarrassed by their bluntness, but I think it's perfect. My family never wanted to talk about anything and look at what a clusterfuck we turned out to be. Shit, I'm so messed up about what the fuck I'm feeling for Kelley that I've been hiding from her like a little chickenshit for the past two weeks.

Well that and the fact I have another surprise for her.

But mostly I'm just a pussy. One minute she's driving me insane, and the next I crave to be inside her. It's a goddamn maddening itch I can't seem to fucking scratch and I needed some time alone to get my head on straight.

I look at my reflection in the small mirror hanging on the gray wall to give myself a pep talk.

All right man, just remember who you are. She deserves the best, and that sure as shit isn't you. Be there for her, but when this is over let her get the fuck on with her life.

I stand up tall, feeling like I got this shit locked down, and head out of my home office to find Kelley. She's lying on the living room floor, head resting on a pillow with her feet propped on the coffee table, a bowl of chips balancing on her stomach with a book held up in her hands, blocking her face. I swing myself over the back of the couch and without even looking out from under her book she blurts out, "How do you feel about the name Jamie?"

I angle my face to read the title. *The Complete Book of Baby Names.* "I think it sucks." She pulls the book away from her face to glare at me. "What? I knew someone named Jamie in high school and he was a royal douche," I say matter-of-factly.

She continues to read from the list. "Ok, What about Beckett?"

I shake my head. "I went to kindergarten with a Beckett. He used to steal everyone's animal crackers."

Kelley snorts. "Well we can't set our kid up to be a cookie thief, now can we?"

"Hell no." I motion for the book, and she hands it over. I peruse the list. "Isaac. That could be cool."

"I once worked with a guy named Isaac. He was fired when they found out he was putting trips to the strip club on the company credit card." Kelley props herself up on her elbow, popping a chip in her mouth.

"Fuck, that's a no then." I scan a few more names, suddenly

able to recall every asshole I ever met. "Shit, you never realize how many people you hate until it's time to name your baby."

Kelley bobs her head in agreement. "Seriously."

I flip a few pages in the book. "How about Jordan? Jordan Blake. That has a nice ring to it."

Kelley shakes her head, disapproving. "And who says the baby's last name is going to be Blake?"

I stare at her. "What do you mean, of course it will be."

She shrugs. "I figured he'd have my name."

I close the book. "Are you serious?"

She pops another chip in her mouth. "I want to have the same last name as my kid."

"And you don't think I want the same thing?"

She looks as if the thought never really occurred to her. She goes quiet and starts to get that sad look I can't fucking stand to see. I never thought about how much stuff you have to consider when having a kid. It's like every single choice you make will affect them for the rest of their lives and it's overwhelming as hell. No wonder I prefer not to think about the future too much.

"Hey." I drop the book on the table and move her bowl of chips next to it. "Let's talk about this later. I have something I want to show you." I extend my hand to help her off the floor. She hesitates, but eventually lets me pull her up.

"Close your eyes." She eyes me skeptically. "I'm good at surprises, remember?" I wiggle my eyebrows, trying to dismiss the concerned look on her face. She cracks a smile and finally does as I say. I step behind her and grab her hip with my right hand, covering her eyes with my left to make sure she can't peek. I carefully guide her down the hall past the guest bathroom.

"You better not be showing me some creepy secret sex dungeon or something, Blake. I mean it."

I press my mouth to her ear before whispering, "You know

you'd love it."

As we reach the threshold of my closed office door and I bring us to a stop, I take one deep breath to calm my nerves.

I hope she loves this even more . . .

CHAPTER

twenty

Kelley

"YOU BETTER NOT BE SHOWING me some creepy secret sex dungeon or something, Blake. I mean it."

As I blindly let Ryan lead me, I find myself nervous. The last time he surprised me with the drive-in movie I just about handed my heart right over. But then again, he's been pretty distant ever since he met my parents, and I can't say I blame him—we're a lot to handle.

"You know you'd love it." His warm breath tickles my ear, and damn it if he isn't right. I feel him bring us to a halt and after a second I hear a door open. He removes his hand from my eyes, but keeps one on my hip. "Ok, you can look."

I slowly raise my eyelids, a little afraid of what I'll find. When my eyes finally focus and adjust to what they see, tears immediately well up behind them. Big, fat ones that will surely make me ugly cry—not cute. It takes everything in me not to let them fall as I step into the room.

I immediately know this to be Ryan's office, although it looks completely different. The walls are now painted a light gray with a crisp white trim. In the far corner a white tufted rocking chair sits with a gray knitted blanket draped over the back. On the left wall is a rustic wooden crib with black and white polka-dotted sheets. A few soft-looking stuffed animals are lined up across the back of the crib. Small, white, wooden cloud cutouts adorn the walls and slate gray curtains cover the windows. An antique chandelier hangs from the middle of the ceiling, and a little mobile of clouds, the moon, and stars hangs directly above the crib. A changing table is off to the right, along with a small bookcase filled with an assortment of toys and books.

I let out a small gasp as I slowly take in every last detail. A small side table next to the crib has a simple typewritten quote in a wood frame:

> "don't think. it
> complicates things.
> just feel, and if it
> feels like home, then
> follow its path."
> - r.m. drake

"That's probably the best piece of advice I can hope to give our kid." I hear Ryan's soft voice from behind me. I turn to see him still standing in the doorway, leaning against it with his hands in his pockets. I'm not sure how to read him right now—he looks calm like this is no big deal so I can't figure out what it means. All I *do* know is I want to run and throw my arms around his neck and kiss his perfect, beautiful mouth, but I stop myself in time to realize it's probably not appropriate. It's one thing to kiss him when we're screwing each other silly, when the urge to do so comes from between my legs, but it's another to want to do it when it comes from inside my chest.

"I can't believe you did this. How? . . . When? . . . Why? . . ." I can barely choke out in an incredulous whisper.

"I just figured he could use a cool place to sleep when he gets out. I did most of it while you were at work. I asked Kinsley for help picking out some of the furniture, but I put it all together."

He motions to the black toolbox in the corner of the room and looks so damn proud it makes my heart melt. Ryan and I might never have a chance at love, but if I had any doubts regarding how he feels about our child, they were just hurled out this carefully decorated nursery window.

"But where's all your stuff? Where are you going to work?"

"I put most of it in storage. I can work anywhere with my laptop, plus I have my actual office in town, remember? It's not a big deal."

He brushes it off easily, but deep down I know what a sacrifice this is for him. One he seems more than willing to make for the sake of our son. A small voice inside my head can't help but bitterly add, *"Yeah, he did this for our kid, but it doesn't change how he feels about you."*

Afraid I'll really lose it if I look at Ryan any longer, I make my way to the bookshelf and run my hands over some of the colorful spines. I stop when I see a copy of *Cloudy with a Chance of Meatballs*. "Oh this was one of my favorites as a kid. I read it so much the back cover practically came off."

Ryan reveals, "Actually, that *is* your copy," just as I pull it out to expose a torn and tattered cover. "I asked your mom if she had any of your old stuff when I talked to her last week. She was more than happy to send over a whole box of books. A lot of them are yours."

Crap, now the ugly tears really do fall, but only for a second before another thought dawns on me. "Wait, you talk to my mother?" I stop the tears with a sharp sniffle.

Ryan tries to look cool, but he is so busted. "She asked for my number before she left the other week. She said you don't answer her calls."

I can only shake my head in disbelief. Except I'm really not all that surprised. My mother apparently loves Ryan. As if this could get any more complicated.

I'm suddenly struck with some type of muscle spasm that feels like someone flicking my stomach from the inside. I grab my stomach and freeze. "Oh my god!"

In a flash Ryan is by my side, looking panicked. "What happened? Are you ok?"

"I think I just felt the baby kick." I pause, assessing any further reaction. "Ah! There it is again!" I grab onto Ryan's hand and place it over my belly.

He furrows his brow, clearly not feeling anything, but after a few seconds he flinches in surprise. "Fuck! How cool is that?" Without removing his hand, he looks at me and beams.

My smile must also be a mile wide. "I think he likes his room."

CHAPTER

twenty-one

Twenty-eight Weeks

Ryan

"HOLY. MOTHER. OF. FUCK."

I watch the screen as a slimy, bloody, wrinkled blob emerges from a sacred place that should never, ever look like a disturbing murder scene.

Kelley and I are sitting in a dark room at the health center with about a dozen other couples, watching the most terrifying piece of cinematic cruelty known to man—birth.

I think I'm about to puke, but I can't look away.

Thank god the torture finally ends and the instructor flips on the lights. Except once you've seen it, you can't *unsee* it.

"Well, I hope everyone enjoyed that!" The young, bubbly nurse looks tickled fucking pink to have shown us that monstrosity.

"Are you kidding me?" I blurt heatedly.

The nurse looks caught off guard and tilts her perky little head. "Excuse me?"

"Why the fuck didn't anybody show us this *before* we're about to live it? I mean show that to a fifteen year old and he'll wait until he's ninety to wave his dick at a girl." A majority of the other scared shitless, soon-to-be dads nod furiously in agreement.

Kelley giggles beside me. "Seriously, Brooks. I am so fucking sorry your vag has to go through that." I give her a solemn look, honestly feeling like a complete toolbag to have done this to her. And they expect me to stick my face down there to watch and then cut some umbilical cord shit?

"I assure you that when it's your own child the entire experience is extremely magical. You'll be so focused on your beautiful new baby that you won't even notice all of the yucky stuff." The nurse waves her hand at me dismissively before launching into the next part of the class.

Yeah, fat fucking chance of that, lady.

One long hour later Kelley and I are headed back out to my truck.

"You ok there, Blake? You look a little pale. If you're having second thoughts we can talk about it . . ." Kelley's concerned tone snaps me from my distracted thoughts. If I'm feeling this freaked out, I can't imagine what she's thinking. But I'm also smart enough to know I need to convince her I can handle this enough for the both of us. She has enough to worry about having to push that baby out of her, I don't want her worrying I'm going to flake on her.

"Me? I'm fine." *Fucking terrified.*

"You sure? You seemed pretty worked up in there. I thought that poor nurse was going to cry when you said both *fuck* and *dick* in the same outburst. Or punch you. Either would have been amusing."

I open the passenger door and help her into her seat. "Serves her right. She could have warned us it was going to be so graphic. I'm just saying they should consider using that video in sex ed classes." I close her door and make my way to the driver's side.

"So you're sure you're ready for this?" Kelley asks as I put my keys in the ignition, roaring the truck to life.

"Of course I'm fucking ready." I snicker and pull out of the parking lot.

I'm so not fucking ready.

LATER THAT NIGHT, AFTER KELLEY goes to sleep, I find myself alone in the nursery, swaying back and forth as I sit in the rocking chair. It's dark, the only light coming from the streetlights outside the window. I can't sleep. Every time I close my eyes I picture things from my past . . . things I hate remembering.

Eleven Years Ago

"MAN, I FUCKING NEED TO get laid tonight. Think one of those bitches is willing?"

Johnny nods toward the main house where a party is raging. We're sitting in lawn chairs way out in the backyard, getting wasted, as usual. I take another big swig from the bottle of booze gripped in my hands. I shrug and lay my head back, enjoying the blissful, numbing feeling that overtakes my body.

"You want in?" Johnny motions for me to join, but I shake my head.

"Nah, I'm good. This shit's all I need." My words are already

slurring as I hold up the bottle to take another drink.

"Suit yourself, bro." Johnny downs and tosses his own beer can to the side before stumbling off to a group of girls standing on the back porch.

I have no real concept of time, but a while later I realize my bottle is empty. I hold it upside down with my mouth open underneath, hoping to catch a few last drops. My head is dizzy and my vision is blurred, but I can see the lights from the house in the distance. I push myself out of my chair, wobbling at the sudden shift of my weight.

I stagger to the house and when I get inside I look around, feeling disoriented by the music and the people. I assume things have died down from when we got here, but fuck if I can remember. I see Johnny passed out on the couch with a topless girl sprawled on top of him. I get in his face and loudly ask, "Dude, where the fuck is my sister? I need to go."

The reason I came here in the first place was because I knew Hazel would be here hanging out with her piece of shit friends. She told me to go to hell and stop following her so I decided to get shit-faced instead. That always seems like the best idea. It's the only way to get my mind off shit.

Johnny squints as he tries to open his eyes and groans. "Fuck, I don't know man." He rolls over and passes back out.

I stumble down one of the hallways, trying to find her. Suddenly I hear screaming—that sounds a lot like Hazel—coming from one of the last rooms at the far end of the hall. I push the door open to see Hazel hitting Tristan and screaming at him to leave her alone. She's wearing a tight black mini-dress that is way too fucking short, revealing the fact her back and arms are covered with tattoos. A man who's known as Dougie D sits on the bed with two girls laying next to him, some of his other drug dealer friends off to the side. I can tell they're stoned out of their minds by the way they stare stupidly as if nothing out of the ordinary is going on. I immediately try to tackle Tristan, but trip over my own feet. Fuck, I wish the room would stop spinning.

"What the hell, Blake."

I shuffle to my feet and push him as hard as I can. "Stay the fuck away from her, Sharp, or I'll kick your fucking ass."

"Ryan, stop! Please." Hazel begs as tears stream down her face. "Please, just take me home."

I sway back and forth as I try to steady myself. "Let's fucking go." I try to grab Hazel's arm and make for the door, but Tristan steps in my way.

"There is no way in hell you can drive, Ry. Let me take you guys."

I throw Tristan's arm off of my shoulder. "Fuck you. I don't want you anywhere near her."

I try to fight him off, but he's sober and I'm fucking loaded so clearly he has the upper hand.

I try to remember more from that night and wish I could say it was the worst of it.

But I don't, and it wasn't.

Ten Years Ago

"WELL, RYAN, TODAY'S THE BIG day. You should be proud of how far you've come."

Dr. Setter signs my discharge papers before indicating for me to do the same.

I hesitate for a second, chewing wildly on a piece of cinnamon gum—my new coping mechanism—before scrawling my signature across the bottom of the page. My right knee bobs up and down faster than a jackhammer.

Dr. Setter looks at me before asking, "Nervous?"

I grunt, shifting in my seat. "Gee, how can you tell?"

Dr. Setter removes his glasses. "It's perfectly normal, Ryan. In fact, it's good you feel that way. Many of our patients convince themselves *they don't need rehab in the first place, so it's easy to think getting back out in the real world for the first time is no big deal. The fact that you've come to terms with your alcoholism means you recognize it as a weakness. And as long as you know that, you can beat it."*

"But what if I fuck up again?" I ask, admitting my deepest fear.

"Know that it would be a choice—you can give in, or you can fight. I suggest you choose wisely."

"Clearly I haven't been very good at making the right choices." I chuckle, avoiding Dr. Setter's stare by looking out the window.

"Want my best piece of advice?"

"Hell yeah I do. What have you been holding out on me, doc?"

Dr. Setter chuckles. "My best advice is not to overthink it. You'll drive yourself mad doing that. Just stay strong and go with your gut, Ryan. I'm sure it will eventually get you where you need to go. Don't let anything else control you. What's in here is what matters most." He taps his chest, indicating his heart.

I nod in understanding and shake Dr. Setter's hand, thanking him as I stand up to leave.

As soon as walk out of the clinic I make a promise to myself—I promise that I will never, ever let a weakness control me ever again. I'm stronger than that. Nothing can break me.

I'm startled awake as I shoot up in the rocking chair. It takes a second to realize I even fell asleep. I look around the room and let my eyes adjust to the darkness. A single beam of light comes in from the window, illuminating the wooden crib. I get up and grab one of the stuffed animals sitting inside and think about the fact that soon I will be bringing a kid in here—into my fucked up world. Will I be able to handle it?

Dr. Setter's words come back to me—*Just stay strong and go with your gut, Ryan. I'm sure it will eventually get you where you need to go.*

His advice has worked for me so far. I just hope it's going to be enough this time.

CHAPTER

twenty-two

Thirty-five Weeks

Kelley

"I'M TELLING YOU, LUC, IT'S crazy how it works. The baby comes out all wrinkly and purple, still attached inside with a cord made up of a vein and arteries and shit, and after that's cut this blob on the other end called the after-birth comes sliding out. It's fucking weird, man."

Kinsley looks at me with curious amusement as we overhear Ryan and Lucas talking a few feet away. I roll my eyes. "Ever since we took that six-week childbirth class it's all he talks about. At first I thought he was scared but now it's like he has some morbid fascination with the entire process."

Kinsley laughs. "I think it's sweet he's so involved."

"There's a fine line between sweet and creepy, Kins." I also laugh, secretly knowing that I do find it strangely sweet. But, per usual, I'm trying really hard to keep an emotional distance from the father of my child. Why does he have to be so damn infuriating? One minute he's making me scream in frustration, and the next it's in complete and utter ecstasy.

I look up and call playfully to Lucas, who looks like he might lose his lunch thanks to Ryan's detailed descriptions. "Sure you don't want a kid anytime soon, Luc?"

He swallows thickly before shaking his head. "I'm good. Besides, I want this one all to myself for a while." He comes up behind Kinsley to rest his head on her shoulder, wrapping his arms around her waist. "So, any big plans for the big two-eight next week, Ry?"

I look confusedly at Ryan, who doesn't make eye contact.

"I guess we'll do the usual? Dinner followed by me whooping your ass in pool at The Cue? If you're lucky I'll even let the birthday boy win a game." Lucas teases. "We're away next weekend, but how about the Monday after? All four of us can go and make a night of it."

Ryan nods but we're interrupted as we hear people begin to arrive at the door. Kinsley insisted on throwing me a baby shower, which I really didn't want, but finally agreed to as long as it would be both guys and girls. That way it feels more like a regular social gathering, and hopefully nobody will ask too many personal questions with the opposite sex present. I knew if it was an all-girl party I would get grilled about the details of my relationship with Ryan, which is not something I want to live through.

As Lucas and Kinsley make their way to greet our guests, I hang back with Ryan. "It's your birthday next week?" I ask. He shrugs. I try to keep the hurt out of my voice. "Why didn't you tell me?"

"It's not a big deal, Brooks."

"Well I think it is. We should do something special."

He raises an eyebrow lustfully. "What did you have in mind?"

I playfully slap his shoulder. "I'm serious."

"So am I." He looks at me with such hunger that I'm afraid I might take my clothes off for him right here. Thankfully people come through the door, distracting us both.

Tristan and Hazel arrive first and I immediately pick up on Ryan's annoyance as soon as he sees them together. Hazel walks up to her brother and hugs him. As I say my own hellos, I hear Ryan sharply ask what she's doing with Tristan, to which Hazel replies, "You know how hard it was to get out without Mom knowing where I was going? I needed a ride and called him. Don't give me that look, Ry. I'm not a kid anymore. By the way, Grams says she's sorry she can't make it, but I have a big gift from her in the car."

Ryan doesn't look thrilled, but softens his expression as more people appear. Most are friends, while some are coworkers or work acquaintances. Thankfully my parents couldn't make it, and obviously we didn't even invite Holly. Among the guests currently arriving are my boss, Logan, and even Gemma. Eli was nice enough to host it at his house, and Kinsley decorated the entire place with mint colored balloons, tons of white peonies, and a big banner that reads "Oh, Baby" with a smaller "We can't wait to meet you Caden" sign beneath. (Yes, Ryan and I finally decided on a name that doesn't remind us of any perverts, jerks, or thieves.)

"This place looks great, Kelley. Kinsley did an awesome job. Thanks so much for inviting me." Gemma looks shyly around the room.

"Of course, Gem. Thanks for coming." I notice Gemma looks distracted so I tilt my head to see she's staring at Logan, who is laughing with Tristan and Lucas. His dimples are on full display, making Gemma blush the same shade as her hair.

I smile to myself. Gemma is so sweet and innocent it's almost nauseating to watch. But cute at the same time. I don't think she'd know what to do with a guy like Logan. Or maybe a guy like him wouldn't know what to do with her.

Kinsley distracts us both by calling me over to open presents. Ryan looks about as thrilled as I do to have to sit in front of everyone and make gaga noises over what they bought us, but it's nice of them to be so generous. The least we can do is gush a little.

Ryan and I sit on the couch as Kinsley hands us the first gift from her and Lucas. I pull out the yellow tissue paper from the gift bag that has adorable baby animals and unwrap the tiniest little onesie that says, "If you think I'm cute you should see my Uncle Lucas."

I laugh out loud and hand it to Ryan, who rolls his eyes. "Yeah, right. This shit is going straight in the trash."

"Come on, man. You know it's true." Lucas replies with a snicker.

"Wait, maybe we'll use it as a diaper first." Ryan tosses it back into the bag, but I can tell he's amused.

I pull out the next gift from the bag and pull out various pieces to a bottle kit. "Aww this will be a big help. Thanks, Kins."

Ryan looks at one of the packages skeptically. "A nipple brush?"

"Dude, it's so not what you think." Lucas shakes his head, confirming he originally had the same misguided idea. All the girls in the room laugh while the men look uncomfortable.

By the time we're finished with all the gifts, it's safe to say Caden shouldn't need anything for a while. Between diapers and toys and a stroller—not to mention the fact his closet will be bigger than mine—he is one lucky kid.

Seeing how generous, genuinely happy, and kind everyone is being today also makes me realize I'm pretty lucky, too.

Which makes me feel extremely guilty since I don't deserve any of it.

AFTER A FEW HOURS OF eating and mingling, the party is finally winding down. Lucas, Kinsley, Logan, Tristan, Hazel, Ryan, and I are in the living room. Everyone is cleaning up while I sit on the couch, too tired, stuffed, and sore to move. Nobody would let me help anyway, which makes me feel even guiltier. Ryan is on the couch next to me, resting back with his arms behind his head and his ankles crossed.

Tristan gathers up assorted empty cups and plates from around the room. "Care to help or are you just going to sit there like an asshole?" He directs his glare at Ryan, who looks completely unfazed.

"Nah, I'm good. But you missed some trash over there." Ryan nods to the side table.

"Fuck you, princess. It's not like you're the pregnant one." Tristan grumbles, but picks up the dirty cup Ryan indicated.

"No, but he's half my kid, which means it's my party, too." Ryan stretches out further to make himself more comfortable, purposely egging Tristan on. Hazel and Kinsley giggle at their banter while Lucas and Logan shake their heads.

"Yeah, about that." Tristan motions between Ryan and I. "I still don't get it. Are you sure this isn't all a joke? Be honest with us, bro—you couldn't keep your dick in your pants and knocked her up by accident, didn't you. "

"What the fuck, T?" Lucas jumps in.

Tristan shrugs. "What? I'm just saying, if you're not going to sack it, go home and whack it." Everyone glares at Tristan now, which makes him get defensive. "Come on, you have to admit this whole 'settling down' thing is shady as shit." He makes air quotes when he says the words *settling down*. "We all know Ry is a use 'em and lose 'em kind of guy, and then all of a sudden he's playing house with some random chick out of the blue?"

Before I have time to process what's happening, Ryan is up, hands balled into fists at his sides. He gets in Tristan's face. "You don't know what the hell you're talking about so I suggest you shut your goddamn mouth. It's none of your fucking business what I do or who I do it with, but if I ever hear you refer to Kelley as some random chick ever again I'll kick your fucking teeth in like I should have done years ago."

I've never seen Ryan look so dominating before, and it sort of scares me.

It also kind of thrills me.

As if sensing this could get ugly, Lucas and Logan move to separate them. Tristan studies Ryan's threatening glare before finally backing off. Ryan holds his hands up in surrender as Luc holds him back, indicating he's cool, although I see his jaw is still clenched.

The room is now filled with an awkward silence as tension hangs heavily in the air. I hope my face doesn't give away all the tortured emotions I'm currently feeling. On the one hand I feel exhilarated Ryan just stood up for me like that, but on the other I know Tristan didn't deserve it—he's actually right.

Ryan reaches for my hand and I robotically let him help me to my feet. He grinds out, "We're going," and makes for the front hall. As he leads me out the door I peek back at Kinsley, who gives me a sad yet understanding look. I return it, trying to apologize. I know her and Lucas are going to have to do some major damage control to keep up this lie for us, especially after that outburst, and it's not fair we put them in this position.

Ryan coldly helps me into my seat of the truck, the back of which is filled with all the boxes and gift bags. Without saying a word he gets into the driver's seat, starts up the engine, and peels out of the driveway.

His anger has me too scared to say anything, so we ride home in silence. We get to the apartment and wordlessly unload the baby gifts. Ryan mumbles something about needing to get work done at the office, and stalks back out the door.

We never talk about what happened.

DESPITE THE FACT RYAN SAID he didn't want to make a big deal about his birthday, I really want to make it special for him. When he finally came home after the baby shower incident last week, we both acted like nothing ever happened. But still, I sense some growing resentment. It's like he's mad he had to get into it with Tristan because of me, and I hate that he convinced me to go through with all of this in the first place. This lie is becoming too much of a burden, but I don't know how to get out of it without making things even worse. I'm hoping a birthday surprise will help us forget about it all for a while.

When I told Ryan to take Friday off and pack a bag for the weekend, he gave me a hard time, but finally conceded. Since my growing stomach makes it harder and more uncomfortable for me to be behind the wheel and we have an hour and a half ride ahead of us, I came up with a plan.

"Turn right here. Then make a left at the light."

"You're really not going to tell me where I'm driving—to my own birthday surprise might I add—you're just going to shout directions at me the whole way?" Ryan sounds annoyed, but I know he secretly loves it.

"Yup, so suck it up. You have no choice but to listen to

everything I say for once." I shoot him a triumphant, wicked smile.

It's just around three p.m. by the time we drive past the sign that says, "Welcome to Peyton Cove." Ryan doesn't say much when he sees it, but looks over to me and says, "You might be better at surprises than me, Brooks. Touché." His big, genuine smile tells me it was a good decision to come here. I was a little nervous about how he'd react, but I remembered how he said it was his favorite place as a kid and thought it might be nice for him to experience it again right before he's about to have a son of his own.

I got us a beachfront hotel suite at one of the nicer looking hotels. We check-in and grab a quick bite before walking out to the beach. Being that it's only May, there aren't many tourists around yet, which means we pretty much have the place to ourselves. We walk along the far end of the beach that's lined with a wall of giant rocks, enjoying the surprisingly warm weather. Ryan was right—it's easy to feel wonderfully isolated in a place like this. That makes me think about all of the things—all of the *feelings*—I'd like to run away from. But I have to face them. I don't want to ruin this moment, but we have a lot to talk about.

I finally chance breaking our comfortable silence. "I want you to know I'm sorry for what happened at the baby shower."

Ryan's jaw tenses. "Just drop it, ok?"

"We have to talk about it sometime." We usually never have a problem getting our stuff out in the open, so the fact he's been more distant lately makes me feel even worse.

"It's not your fault, Brooks. Let it go." He continues down the beach, looking annoyed, which irritates me.

"You're right, it's not my fault." I stop walking and look at him, the anger I've been feeling for weeks finally coming to the surface at his refusal to face things. "It's *both* our faults."

Ryan stops a few steps ahead of me. He takes a deep breath before turning back to face me. "Do we really have to get into this now?"

"Yes, we do. Because I'm sick of this. I'm sick of feeling like this lie is getting too big for us. We started this whole thing to keep anyone from getting hurt, but I feel like that's all we're doing. It was fucking selfish, Ryan." He offers nothing to the contrary, so I cross my arms and continue. "It was idiotic enough to lie, but then we had to go and drag Kinsley and Lucas into it, forcing them to cover for us. They're supposed to be our best friends." I shake my head in disgust, talking faster as I get worked up. "Everything had to go and get so complicated. We both know this isn't going to last, but you have to go and do things like take me on dates and build a nursery. You don't think that confuses the hell out of me? It's a sick reminder of the life we'll never have together. I'm still wearing your grandmother's ring and you talk to my mother more than I do, for Christ's sake. Like it or not, both our families are involved and I just don't see how this can still work like we planned."

"What do you want me to do, Kell? I'm fucking trying here." Ryan's tries to keep his voice calm, but I can tell he's just as frustrated. "Can't we agree on some way to fix this?"

"We can't even agree on what last name our baby is going to have!" I laugh, even though it's not funny. "But the real kicker? Oh, the real kicker is that you just got into a fight with one of your closest friends to defend our relationship when he was the only one telling the fucking truth!" I sink down to sit on one of the large rocks. My feet and back are tired. Hell, my head and heart are tired, too.

I drop my head, trying to calm down when I notice Ryan drop to one knee in front of me. I look at him, confused.

"Marry me." It's a statement more than a question.

"What?" I ask, positive I heard him wrong.

"I know we fucked this up a long time ago, and I know we'll probably still fuck it up in the future, but if I learned one thing these past few months it's that I really fucking like you, Brooks. A lot. I want to have this baby with you, and I want us both to be there to mess up his life equally. You're right, this whole situation is both our faults, so let's make it right. Let's stop pretending, let's give this kid the same last name, and let's turn this lie into a truth. Right here, right now. For real this time."

My heart beats so fast and so loud I can feel it ringing in my ears. I barely notice the tears running down my cheeks. I feel such a mixture of disbelief and excitement that I start to laugh. All I can manage to blurt out is, "That proposal is almost as bad as your first."

Ryan looks at me with a lopsided smile. "Is that a yes?"

I take a deep breath, needing a second to clear my head.

I let out a sigh. "Why, Ryan? Why me? If it's just because we're having a baby together you can forget it." I can't deny my feelings for Ryan have grown over the past few months, but he was very clear and up front about his lack of commitment skills. Is he just doing this because he feels like he has no other choice?

Ryan moves to sit next to me on the rock, grabbing my chin with his fingers to force me to look into his eyes. "You've been different from the very beginning, Kelley. Ever since I first met you, you did things to me I didn't understand. I didn't want to understand. Yes, this baby is what brought us into this situation, but if not for him we never would have had the chance to get to know each other. And I'm so fucking thankful we did. I'm not used to any of this, but I know if there is one person I want by my side as I figure it out, it's you. Let's forget about everything and everyone else and see where this goes. I'll go get a justice of the peace right now and marry the shit out of you right here.

Let's stop overthinking all the bullshit and just do it. Let's just commit to being together and give our family a shot. Can we at least agree on that?"

As much as this may not be the proposal I always dreamed of, I can't deny it still somehow feels perfect. I think about how I always pictured a fancy wedding with a flowing white dress and a room full of people to witness it all. Then I think about my dad's words: *If you love someone and want to marry her, you should just do it . . . let it be about the two of you—the only people who matter.*

For once I don't want to think. I just want to feel. And it feels so infuriatingly good to feel wanted . . . and to know that I want him right back.

Without thinking I look into Ryan's fierce, beautiful face and say, "Ok, Ryan Bartholomew Blake—let's get married."

CHAPTER

twenty-three

Ryan

"OK, RYAN BARTHOLOMEW BLAKE—LET'S GET married."

I never thought a few simple words could make me feel like such a fucking sappy shit, but hearing Kelley Brooks agree to marry me almost has me fist pumping like a damn fool. I think I was more surprised than Kelley to hear the words come out of my mouth, but once they did I noticed I didn't want to take them back.

Not wanting to waste time—or give either of us a chance to overthink our decision—I help Kelley stand and jog us a few yards down the beach until we reach the small town square. I glance around until I see a building marked *Town Hall* and pull us up the steps and through the front door. It's almost four, which means they'll be closing soon. I scan the directory for the clerk's office and make our way to the second floor. An older woman sits alone behind the desk, looking like she's getting ready to pack it in for the day. Her name placard reads *Marge Brown*.

"Excuse me, I was wondering if my fiancée here and I could get a marriage license?" I smile excitedly.

The woman looks at us and smiles back, routinely launching into a spiel about what documentation she needs to see and how it takes three days to approve.

I muster my sweetest, most charming voice. "Look, I know you're just doing your job and I'm sure there's a very good reason they make these rules, but as you can see we're a little pressed for time." I gesture to Kelley's large, round stomach. I see Marge's eyes go soft and I know I've got her on the hook. "We're only in town for a short time and we really, really have our hearts set on getting married on this beach today." I reach in my pocket and pull out my driver's license. "As you can see, today is my birthday, and the only gift I want is to marry the mother of my child. So what do you say, Marge, do you think you can help us out?" She looks torn as her eyes tear up, so I lay on the sad puppy dog eyes to seal the deal.

"Oh well isn't that just the sweetest thing I've ever heard." Marge sniffles back a few tears and grabs a few papers from the filing cabinet next to her. "I'll need both of your driver's licenses and then fill out this form here, here, and here. I'll be sure to have this expedited."

I smile triumphantly and begin to fill out the forms. "Now, any chance you know a justice of the peace?"

AN HOUR LATER KELLEY AND I are standing on the beach, hands linked, just us, the waves, and Edward Brown—thank fucking god Marge's husband is a JP.

I'm not going to lie, there was a moment there when I thought I lost my fucking mind. I mean, me . . . get married?

Really settle down and have the kid and wife and fucking Sunday pancake breakfasts or some shit?

But standing here, looking at Kelley . . . her brown hair messy from the wind, wearing fucking stretchy maternity pants and a red long-sleeved shirt that hugs her round curves, her fucking gorgeous, intense eyes looking at me with such hope and trust . . . fuck. In this moment I know I love her, and I've loved her ever since I claimed her on the floor of that damn storage shed.

And the thought fucking terrifies me, because I've never said those words to anyone in my life. I don't know that I can. Feeling is one thing, but actually admitting it out loud? Love is a weakness. What if she doesn't feel the same . . . what if this is only about appearances for her?

Edward's deep voice pulls me back to the present moment as we begin.

"This is an important moment—it's a celebration of love, commitment, friendship, and family. We have thousands of important moments that happen in our lives, though, so what makes this special? Why this moment? Because it's a collective, passionate breath signifying two people who are in it for forever. Because despite any differences, love is what we share. It's the great unifier, our one universal truth. No matter who we are, where we come from, or what we believe, we know this one thing: love is what we're doing right. And even though this experience is so incredible, words fail us when we try and explain it. That's just the way it is with love—it's meant to be felt, not described. But even though we still try to describe love in different ways—and even though love can look different—we all know it when we see it. And we see it here. You fell in love by chance, but you're here today because you're making a choice. You're choosing each other. And so it is the most profound moment you can ever hope to experience."

As the sun sets, I know that this is in fact the best choice and the best moment of my entire life.

"Do you, Ryan Blake, promise to keep Kelley Brooks as your favorite person—to laugh with her, surprise her, support her through life's tough moments, kill spiders for her, grow old with her, and find new reasons to love her every day?"

There's no question. No hesitation. Just truth. "I do."

We didn't have time to get rings, so I slip a small loop of twine around her finger.

"And do you, Kelley Brooks, promise to keep Ryan Blake as your best friend—to laugh with him, comfort him through good & bad times, have sex with him in showers, always sleep naked with him, grow a family with him, and find new reasons to love him every day?"

. . . I may have asked him to add one or two things to Kelley's vows. By the way happy tears trail down her cheeks and a smile lights up her face, I'd say she doesn't mind.

Without ever breaking her gaze from mine, Kelley whispers softly, but surely, "I do." She slips a matching piece of twine on my finger.

"I now pronounce you husband and wife. Ryan, you may ki—"

I can't wait another second to feel Kelley's sweet, maddening lips on mine. I knew from my very first taste nine months ago that I would get addicted as fuck. But hell, I'll gladly be a Kelley Brooks addict for the rest of my friggin' life. It would be my pleasure.

And hers.

As soon as our lips collide my heart beats wildly against my ribs. No wonder it needs a fucking cage. I feel desperate and determined to keep this woman forever. Longer than forever.

Everything I told her today was true, more than I even knew until the words came spilling out. But the choice to marry her was clear and unmistakable. I want this. I want her.

Even if I can't say it, I plan to show her just how much I fucking care. It may not be the fairytale she imagined, but I promise to spend the rest of my life trying to be the best version of myself I can be. Just call me Ryan Fucking Charming.

By the time we finally break our kiss, the sun is almost fully set and Edward is nowhere to be found. For a split second I think I dreamt the whole thing, so I reach out to cup Kelley's face. I feel her warm skin beneath my palm, reassuring me that this is real.

She looks at me with a shy smile. "That really happened."

"Yeah, babe, it did." I rest my forehead on hers.

She blushes and looks so goddamn beautiful that I can't wait any longer to get her alone and bury myself inside her. I grab her hand and pull her toward our hotel.

As soon as we get inside our room I pin her against the back of the door, careful not to hurt her or the baby, but feeling like a fucking animal. Her soft whimpers have me pulling back, realizing she deserves more than some quick fuck against the door. She deserves to be fucking worshipped, and that's exactly what I plan to do. I may not be able to tell her I love her yet, but I can sure as shit show her.

I press one last kiss to her lips before slowing down and leading her to the foot of the king sized bed. I let my hands explore her body before I pull off her shirt and slide down her pants, needing to see every unexposed part of her. When I have her completely bare before me it's as if all the air is sucked from my lungs. Never before has the thought of a pregnant chick done anything for me, but seeing *this* pregnant chick—*my wife*—carrying our child, an entire person only the two of us could have created together . . . well let's just say my dick approves. *A lot.*

I kneel before her and press a kiss to her right ankle, slowly making my way up her body, kissing across every inch of her skin. When I get to her lips, I slide my tongue across them, craving her fucking intoxicating taste. She moans into my mouth before desperately begging, "Please Ryan. I need you. All of you."

I remove my own clothes and guide her to lay on the bed. I crawl up to spoon her small body. From this position I can support her leg, which I lift to angle myself at her entrance from behind. I kiss her shoulder and the spot right at the base of her neck, whispering that she's mine. I slowly push myself inside her, taking my time to feel every inch of her. She feels even more incredible than ever before. I don't know that I can say I ever made love to a woman before, but if it's always like this, I'll give up merely fucking for the rest of my life. But I know this is an experience I'll only ever get to share with Kelley Brooks.

No longer able to hold back, I grip her thigh, stretching her wider, and thrust deeper. Her moans let me know she's more than ok with it. I continue my pace until I feel her muscles contract, and a pleasured cry falls from her lips. I allow myself to let go a second later, burying my face in her neck. Once we both have a chance to recover, I move to lay on the opposite side, needing to look into her eyes. A satisfied smile spreads across her lips as her eyelids get heavy. I pull the covers over us and wrap her in my arms. Once I hear her breath go slow and steady, I kiss her forehead and run my fingers over her stomach, tracing a distinct straight line, two arches with a point, and a curve.

I <3 U

CHAPTER

twenty-four

Kelley

OH MY GOD. WHAT HAVE I done?

I bolt up in bed, the events of last night replaying in my head. The last thing I remember is falling asleep in Ryan's arms.

Oh, and that was after we got married and had the most amazing sex ever.

What the hell is wrong with me?

Marrying Ryan Blake was *not* part of the plan. Our situation was meant to be short-lived . . . it was supposed to be fake. There is no way what we did last night is right. I mean the man has never even said he loves me and I went and fucking married him. I got so caught up in our pretend relationship that I couldn't think straight. I've just wanted this for so long . . . the family, the marriage, the husband . . .

But not like this. Not when our entire relationship has been based on a lie. There is no way he really loves me—it must be a game to him. A challenge. He's never even been in a relationship and now he thinks he can take on being a father *and* a husband? And what will happen to me—to our son—when Ryan realizes he made a mistake? So he threw some of his money around to decorate a nursery and he charmed my parents into liking him— big fucking deal. That doesn't actually prove he has feelings for *me*. There is, after all, a reason he's always kept women at a distance. Why would I be any different in the end? Forever is a long time to promise someone who was meant to be temporary.

I knew it was dangerous to get too close to Ryan Blake. I knew I would fall for him a little more every single minute of being around him, despite the fact he is not even close to being Mr. Right. And then he had to go and say all sorts of shit I wanted— and needed—to hear last night that I let myself believe it was right. But it's not. I can't do this.

I look over to see that Ryan is still sleeping, and immediately slide myself out of bed. I grab my clothes and dash to the bathroom, locking the door behind me. I pull on my pants and shirt and stare at my reflection in the mirror.

You, Kelley Brooks, are an idiot.

I know I have to get out of here as soon as possible, so I slip out of the bathroom, attempting to hold back tears as I simultaneously try to quiet the tiny voice inside my head that's telling me I'm just scared to admit I actually love him . . . that somehow what we have is real. Love shouldn't be scary, though, right? It should be wonderful and magical, not some secret, rushed affair on a secluded beach in the middle of nowhere. That's not real life, no way.

I scribble a quick message on the hotel notepad sitting on the side table, grab my things, and quickly, but quietly, leave the room. I move as fast as my swollen, pregnant legs will carry me, grabbing my cell out of my bag to call a cab as I make my way outside.

A COUPLE OF HOURS LATER the cab pulls up to Ryan's apartment. I wipe my eyes with the back of my hand. I cried silent tears the whole ride home.

Home.

No matter how much I want to believe that's what this place has been for the past nine months, I don't belong here. I never did.

I'm hoping I have enough of a head start to grab my things and my car keys before Ryan even discovers I left. I make a bee-line for the elevator and let myself into the apartment. I go to the bedroom where I throw some clothes in a bag before heading back down the hall to leave. As I make my way to the kitchen I rifle through my purse to find my keys. I finally find them and reach for the front door when I find myself face to face with the most intense, angry blue eyes I've ever seen.

"Care to tell me what the fuck this is about, Brooks?"

CHAPTER

twenty-five

Ryan

"CARE TO TELL ME WHAT the fuck this is about, Brooks?"

I hold up the scrap of paper I woke up to find beside my empty hotel bed and place it on the counter.

Last night was a mistake. I'm sorry.

Kelley looks nervous as she places her bag on the floor. *She fucking packed a bag already?*

She looks sadly at the note and lets out a deep sigh before saying, "We both know it's true . . . we got caught up and took things a little too far."

I cross my arms, challenging her. "And which part was the mistake, exactly? Marrying me or begging me to fuck you?"

She winces at my harsh words, but I don't care. I want everything out in the fucking open. When I woke up to find she had

left . . . fuck. Let's just say it's been a long time since I felt aban-
doned. This is what happens when I give in and let a weakness
get the better of me.

Her voice hardens as she gathers her resolve. "That's not
fair, and you know it. Jesus, Blake, you don't even love me!"

She looks at me with such fucking sad, wounded eyes I'm
caught off guard. "What the fuck? Of course I do."

"Then say it."

I pretend I don't know what she's talking about. I hate feeling this out of control. She's never said it either, so what if she's
trying to play some sick fucking mind games? "Say what?"

She throws me an accusatory glare. "This is what I mean.
We had a deal and you had to go and mess it all up."

Afraid I might lose my fucking mind, I instinctively get defensive. "Oh, so now it's all my fucking fault. If that's the case
why bother apologizing?" I toss her note angrily on the kitchen
counter.

She stares at me powerfully and steels her fists before shouting, "Because I am sorry. I'm sorry I moved in with you, I'm sorry we lied to everyone, and I'm sorry we pretended to be together. But most of all I'm sorry I ever screwed you on that stupid
fucking storage shed floor in the first place!"

Her words feel like a sharp knife to my gut. I grind my teeth
together, trying to stop the pain from tearing through my chest.
"I never forced you to stay. If you didn't want this you should
have said so."

"Well I'm saying it now! I need love, Ry, true love, not whatever we have . . . this just hurts. If I want to give fate a chance I
have to stop messing around by pretending this fake relationship
means something more."

That makes me grunt sarcastically before raising my own
voice to shout. "Fate could be pounding down your fucking door,

Kell, but you'd be too busy dreaming to even hear it. Although apparently unless a guy is riding some sissy fucking white horse it means nothing. You think that shit is real? Maybe love is supposed to fucking hurt and that's how you know it's real." I motion between us. "We're real. This is real. You spout all this bullshit about true love but I don't think you even know what that fucking means." I turn and grip the back of my head, frustrated she can be so blind to what's right in front of her. If I can see it, why the hell can't she? Maybe I haven't been the best about verbally expressing my feelings, but haven't my actions proven anything?

Things get real quiet before I hear her speak in a near whisper behind me. "You just think it's real because we've been pretending for so long we can't tell where the lie ends and the truth begins."

I hear a soft *clink* before the door opens and closes with a final *thud*.

I turn to find my grandmother's ring resting on the cold, bare counter next to a loop of twine. That, along with the torment of her words ringing in my ears, keeps me from going after her. I put my heart on the fucking line only to have it ripped to shreds. She doesn't want me. She doesn't want *us*. Why should she? I was an asshole to think I could be different for her. My half-assed attempt at love wasn't enough, and I don't fucking blame her for wanting more. I let my guard down to give into some sweet, sick craving, and, like all addicts, am left with nothing but pain. Pain I feel, pain I caused. My past finally caught up to me and in the end my son will grow up without a father just like I tried to avoid in the first place. *Great fucking job, Blake.*

I storm into the kitchen and tear open the top cabinet, tossing shit aside until I find the one thing I'm looking for buried in the back. I forcefully break the seal on the bottle of Jack and pour a generous amount into a glass. Desperate to do anything that will numb the fucking throbbing agony twisting deep in the pit of my chest, I bring the cup to my lips. At the last second before it reaches my tongue, I catch a glimpse of my damaged reflection rippling through the bottom of the amber liquid. *Fuck!* I pull my arm back and violently throw it with full force against the kitchen wall. With my head in my hands I slink down amidst the broken glass, letting the liquor pool on the floor around me.

CHAPTER

twenty-six

Kelley

AS SOON AS THE DOOR closes behind me, I can't help but feel like I've made yet another huge mistake. I look down to my naked finger, which makes the pit of my stomach feel hollow.

No, it's not real . . . it can't be real. Ryan Blake plus Kelley Brooks do not equal a happily ever after.

As much as I wanted to believe differently, they just don't.

I head to the elevators, needing to put as much distance between Ryan and I as possible. It's the only way out of this.

When I enter the lobby I see Darrin smiling. I try to hide my red, splotchy face from view but it's no use.

As he comes over to help me as I struggle with my bag he can immediately tell I'm upset. "Hey hun, what's wrong?"

All it takes is his big, warm hand on my shoulder and sympathetic eyes staring at me to cause a full on breakdown. A fresh wave of tears stream down my cheeks, and this time they're loud, ugly, and blubbering.

Darrin's face clouds with concern as he tries to soothe me, pulling me into a giant bear hug. "Oh boy. It's ok. Hey, now . . . there, there."

I take a few gulps of air, trying to regain some semblance of composure as I realize how embarrassing this is. It doesn't help Darrin's shirt is now soaked with my tears. And probably some snot too.

With one hand he reaches for his handkerchief and slips it to me between us. I nod into his chest to indicate my gratitude and blow my nose. Loudly. Once my all-out sobs turn to a mild whimper, Darrin cautiously releases me.

"You want to tell me what happened?"

I shake my head. "It's all so complicated. This isn't how my life is supposed to turn out. I'm supposed to meet the right guy, fall in love, get married, and start a family, not be pregnant *while* getting married and *then* fall in love." I sniffle at the absurdity of the situation.

Darrin must be confused as hell, but thankfully he doesn't show it. He just pats my cheek and says, "That's what always screws us up the most, isn't it? Picturing what should or could have been. You can't live your life with a bunch of what-ifs. The best you can do is wake up every day and ask yourself, 'Am I happy?' If the answer is no, you do something to change it. But if it's a yes, well then you go on and let yourself be happy."

His simple way of looking at the world fascinates me. Can it really be that easy?

"I don't think I can do that." I admit truthfully.

"Sure you can. Isn't that why you were with Ryan in the first place—because he makes you happy?"

He eyes me with an expectant smirk. I look down at my feet, not wanting to think about how Ryan makes me feel. "I don't know," I whisper.

Darrin reaches down to pick up my bag and holds it out to me. He says in a serious yet playful tone, "Well then that's probably the first thing you need to figure out."

CHAPTER

twenty-seven

Thirty-seven Weeks

Ryan

THIRTY-SIX.

There are thirty-six things in this room that remind me of Kelley.

It's been thirty-six hours since I've seen her.

It took me thirty-six weeks to realize I loved her.

And it took about thirty-six seconds to lose her when she walked out the door.

I fucking hate the number thirty-six.

A knock at the door pulls me from my thoughts. I debate answering, but the pounding gets louder, pissing me off. I get off the couch and violently swing open the door to reveal Lucas and Kinsley.

I don't even bother saying anything. I just turn and stalk back to the couch, muttering *"Fucking great,"* under my breath.

They follow me in anyway, and Lucas asks, "You ready to go?"

"Go where?" I bite, having no clue what the fuck he's talking about.

"Out for your birthday dinner, smartass. Now where's Kelley? I'm starved."

Lucas starts looking around the apartment and I want to hit something. I clearly forgot about tonight and I sure as shit don't feel like celebrating. "She's not fucking here. I have shit to do to-night anyway so you guys can just go."

They obviously pick up on my not-so-subtle shitty attitude, but before Luc can give me crap for it Kinsley steps in. "Did something happen with Kelley?"

"No, it's just fucking over is all. Hell, it was never anything to begin with. The point is she left, and I'm busy tonight so can we do this some other time?"

"Dude, what the hell? It's not like you to be so goddamn pis-sy." I can tell Lucas is concerned, even if he doesn't sound it.

But I'm so fucked up over everything that's happened the only way I know how to react is to snap. "You don't know shit about me."

Most people would leave at this point, but Lucas knows me well enough not to be bothered by my rare outbursts. "Well, well. Look whose turn it is to be heartbroken." He turns toward Kinsley saying, "Sorry, babe—I'm glad we're good now," before grinning back at me. He must be referring to the fact he couldn't get out of bed when Kinsley kicked his ass to the curb last year.

"Fuck you. At least I'm not pretending to be sick like some kind of pussy. The door's over there, asshole."

Lucas just laughs. "Payback's a bitch."

I glare at him before Kinsley steps between us. "Ok guys, put 'em back in your pants." She presses a quick kiss to Lucas' lips before saying, "How about you go wait in the car? I'll be right down."

Luc looks like he wants to protest, but nods in agreement before heading out the door. Before he leaves he calls back, "I know how much you must be hurting so I'm going to forgive you for being such a dick. But you better be nice to my wife or I'll have to kick your ass."

I grunt as the door closes behind him. I try to avoid Kinsley's stare. Lucas I can deal with, but Kinsley? I have a feeling she knows how to see right through me.

She plops down on the couch next to me before joking, "So that whole control thing . . . it's working out well for you I see."

I chance glancing over to her, and see she's trying not to laugh. I throw my head back against the couch. "Shit." I look back to her before admitting, "It's fucking harder than it looks."

"Trust me, I know. You're preaching to the choir with that one."

"So what am I supposed to do? This fucking sucks."

Kinsley chews her lip as if contemplating what to say. Finally she simply states, "You decide to let go. It's scary at first, but you learn it's not so bad. And it's worth it if it means you finally get what you want."

"And what if what you want is also what scares the shit out of you?" I ask, dead serious.

"That's usually how you know it's something really good. What scares us makes us stronger, right?" I shrug, not sure what to say. Kinsley's voice gets softer before continuing, "Look, Luc told me you haven't had the easiest past, and trust me I know what it's like to feel like you're defined by all the shitty things you went through; like that means you deserve a shitty life. But it doesn't have to be that way, Ry. You just need to confront the past and realize it doesn't have to control your future."

She squeezes my shoulder before getting up to leave. I know what she's saying is probably really fucking smart, but for some reason all I can focus on is her talking about confronting the past. In my irritated state, I suddenly have the urge to not only confront my past, but punch it in the fucking balls.

TWO HOURS LATER I'M PULLING up to a huge house three towns over. It only took a quick internet search to find out where Richard Blake lives, and knowing he's lived so close this whole time without ever trying to contact me or my sister only fuels my determination to face him.

I ring the doorbell and shove my hands in my pockets, steeling myself so I don't completely lose my shit.

A few seconds later the door opens to reveal an older looking man in khaki pants and a blue button up shirt. I catch a whiff of bourbon and am immediately transported back to my ten-year-old self. I've pictured my dad's face many times over the years—how I thought I remembered it—and am surprised to see it is spot on. Only his hair is grayer and more lines slice across his wrinkled forehead.

"Can I help you?" he asks, completely unaware of who I am, which makes me laugh.

Without moving I ask calmly, "You can tell me why the fuck you walked out eighteen years ago."

"Ryan?" He sighs and avoids looking me in the eye as recognition finally dawns on him, but I don't back down. He rubs the back of his neck, a gesture I'm disturbed to realize I inherited. "What do you want me to say, son? It was a long time ago."

Hearing this stranger call me son fuels the fire. "So that's it.

There was no actual reason for you to abandon your family? You were just able to walk away and never look back, easy as that?" I squeeze my fists shut and feel all the pent up anger I've carried with me for the past eighteen years burn behind my eyes.

"I'm sorry it happened that way, but it was what was best for me. I wasn't happy and I needed a fresh start. I don't know what else you want me to tell you. It was easier to leave it all behind; it wasn't worth the fight to get into it with your mother."

He shrugs weakly and looks like a complete coward, allowing me to understand with absolute certainty that while I might share some physical traits with the guy, I am nothing like him. Not in any way that matters. Because I know I could never, ever walk away from my son for my own selfish reasons. From the moment Kelley told me she was pregnant, my life became about her and my kid and no matter what crap has happened between us that has never changed. Even if Kelley and I aren't meant to be together, my family will always be worth any shit I have to go through. It's not about what's easiest, it's about what's right. If Kelley needs me, then I'll fucking be there. No questions, no hesitation. If giving her space is what is best for her then I'll fucking do it even if it rips my heart out. But I'm also not going down without a fight.

And this, I suddenly realize, is exactly what love is. It's not a fucking weakness, it's a privilege. One my father lost a long time ago. One that I hopefully still have time to earn back.

I shake my head and snicker, "Thanks, dad."

"For what?" he asks, rightfully unsure.

"For showing me what kind of father not to be." Without hesitation I turn and head back to my truck, never once looking back.

My dad fucked up, but that's his shit to deal with. There is no use comparing myself to him or wondering what could have been. That shit is in the past, and that's where it's going to stay. If I walk away from Kelley and Caden now then I'd be just as bad as him, but I know I won't. All I need to worry about now is taking care of my own family and screw everybody else. When life stands there and grabs you by the balls, beating the ever-living shit out of you, you can either pussy out and run from it or you can pick yourself up off the floor and accept the challenge. And I fully intend to look that fucker in the face and tell it to go to hell.

I just hope it's not too late.

CHAPTER

twenty-eight

Thirty-eight Weeks

Kelley

I THOUGHT TIME AWAY FROM Ryan would help get him off my mind.

Boy was I wrong.

A few days after I left his apartment I went to the office thinking I could throw myself into work in order to forget him. As soon as I walked in I saw the final, signed lease agreement for *Grind* on my desk. I walked right back out and called in my maternity leave.

The next day I stayed on the couch with a tub of ice cream, determined to watch nothing but sappy chick flicks and bawl my eyes out. The first channel I flipped to was playing *The Princess Bride* so I turned off the tv and tried not to puke instead.

Two days after that I swear the mailman smelled like cinnamon, so I shut myself in my room and have successfully avoided any type of human contact for the past few days.

Now it's three a.m. and I can't stop tossing and turning, unable to get comfortable. My bed feels too empty. My apartment feels empty. My fucking life feels empty. I have nothing, except for this baby growing inside me, which is now bittersweet.

The good news is I will always have a piece of Ryan Blake to hold onto.

The bad news is I will always have a piece of Ryan Blake to hold onto.

I find myself wishing our son's eyes will be the same shade of blue as his dad's, but I know that would also break my heart. I have enough trouble getting images of them out of my head as it is. First I see them looking intense and sincere as he vowed to spend forever with me, and then I think about how wild and lost they were when I told him it was all a mistake. That *we* were a mistake.

Except that was a lie—ironically the first one I ever told him. Not only is Ryan the father of my child, but he's also my best friend . . . and that is something I didn't expect to mean so much to me. I would do it all over again if it meant we could be together, even knowing how painful it would turn out in the end.

For the past two weeks I've done nothing but replay every moment we spent together, trying to understand where exactly it went so completely wrong. Looking back it seems like I had everything, but at the time it felt like nothing. I didn't want him to choose me because he had to. I wanted so much more with him . . . I wanted everything.

He thinks I left because I don't love him? I left because I love him too fucking much.

And that's the sad, harsh, ironic truth—a lie brought us

together, and the truth tore us apart.

The pain I feel in my heart suddenly shoots across my abdomen, making me double over. It feels like someone has my insides in a tight vise and then it releases.

I swing my legs over the side of the bed when I'm hit with another wave of spine tingling pressure that makes me cry out. I grip the side table to steady myself as I try to stand. When I look back I notice a red stain on the sheets. Panic grips me as I fear the worst—I'm not due for another couple of weeks. This can't be happening. Not again.

Cradling my stomach in my hands, I reach for my cell phone. As the phone rings on the other line I whisper to my belly, "Please Caden. Hang in there. I promise to take care of you and love you more than anything just please be ok. I need you to be ok."

Finally the call picks up and amidst another round of sharp pain I grind out, "Kins, I need to get to the hospital. I think I'm about to have this baby."

FIFTEEN MINUTES LATER LUCAS AND Kinsley pick me up and I spend the entire ride to the hospital yelling at Lucas to drive faster.

"I'm already going forty over the speed limit. Unless you want to get there by ambulance you're going to have to chill out."

I called Dr. Conners as soon as I got off the phone with Kinsley, and while she told me a little spotting is typically normal, I'm anxious to make sure everything is ok.

I'm about to make some crack about my grandma driving faster than this, but Kinsley pipes in and squeezes my hand reassuringly. "We're almost there, Kells, promise."

When we get to the hospital entrance a nurse comes out with a wheelchair. Kinsley and Lucas follow as I'm wheeled into the waiting room. As we round the corner I hear shouting. I look up to see Ryan at the nurse's station, looking like he's about to deck someone.

I glare at Lucas, even though I'm secretly relieved. Of course he called him.

Ryan spots me and he rushes over as I'm hit with the worst pain I've ever experienced in my life. I try to breathe through it, but it fucking hurts.

The nurse looks at me before stating, "We need to get you into a room right away. Your friends can wait here."

She starts to wheel me down the hall and Ryan follows closely behind. Since we barely acknowledge each other and I don't offer an explanation, the nurse holds him back. "Sir, I'm sorry, you can wait here."

Ryan looks at me, unsure, and I become anxious as another agonizing contraction rips through me so I loudly confess, "He's my husband!"

I don't miss Lucas and Kinsley's shocked and confused expressions, but I can't deal with that right now. I'm being ripped apart from the inside out and regardless of whatever happened between us, Ryan is the only person I want with me in that delivery room.

The nurse helps me change into a gown and a short while later Dr. Conners appears. All I keep repeating is, "How's the baby? Is he ok?" That's the only thing that matters. I already lost one Blake boy . . . losing the other would destroy me.

I look restlessly at Ryan, fear and panic blazing in my eyes. He kisses my forehead and squeezes my hand. Dr. Conners assures me everything is fine, and I burst into tears.

The next surge of crippling pain pulls me back to the

situation at hand, and I get the overwhelming urge to push. I hear the doctor say something about ten centimeters and the nurse coaches me on how to breathe through each contraction. Every time I feel one hit I take a deep breath and push with all of my might for about ten seconds, then relax until the next strikes a moment later.

Funnily enough, I can't help but think labor is a lot like being in love: It starts out all great and happy . . . you're excited about what's going to happen and think everything will be sunshine and rainbows from here on out, but then reality—no doubt coupled with pain—eventually kicks in, swiftly and suddenly, and it takes everything in you to get through it. You feel drained and weak, positive you can't go on, but somehow you survive, and all you can do is take deep breaths and try to push the feelings aside. And while you might get some small glimmer of temporary relief, just as you begin to relax, the hurt hits you out of nowhere yet again, causing you to scream in agony.

I grind my teeth together and bear down as hard as I can as the next wave of torment crashes into me, thinking I deserve every single ounce of misery coming to me.

The next hour passes in a blur as I experience just about every emotion humanly possible—fear, pain, excitement, anxiety, more pain, and relief. But as soon as they lay my son on my chest time passes in slow motion and everything goes quiet as the most profound sense of complete and utter amazement overtakes me. I know without a doubt this fascinating being we created was more than worth every ounce of pain I had to endure. I look up to Ryan, who runs his hand down my shoulder and kisses Caden's forehead, smiling bigger than I ever thought possible, and I know loving him was worth it, too.

I just wish he could love me back.

And just like that everyone and everything in the room

resumes its normal pace as noise and excitement fill the air. After Caden's cleaned and wrapped I get to hold him for a while before exhaustion overtakes me and I finally drift off to sleep.

WHEN I FINALLY OPEN MY eyes, I see Ryan standing at the foot of the bed. He's wearing the same worn pair of jeans and purple t-shirt he had on yesterday. His hair looks adorably messy, like he spent all night running his fingers through it. While he's never exactly been hard on the eyes, the way he looks holding our son—strong and proud—steals the air from my lungs. When he notices I'm awake he smiles, and the sight has my throat choking up.

Needing to focus on anything else I ask in a raspy voice, "So, was the nurse right?" He raises a quizzical eyebrow. "Was birth magical to watch since it was your own kid?" I tease, pushing myself against the pillows to sit up.

He rocks Caden back and forth, stroking the tops of his tiny fingers. "I didn't think it was possible to feel so much for someone you just met until they put this little guy in my arms." He pauses to look at me and chuckles. "But it was still fucking gross."

I laugh out loud before extending my arms. "Ok, my turn. Hand him over."

Ryan comes around to the side of the bed and places Caden in my lap. I stare down into his soft, sleepy face, fully aware he looks just like his dad. *Fuck my life.*

After a moment of awkward silence Ryan clears his throat. "Kelley, I—"

I cut him off before he has the chance to say anything. "Please, Blake. Don't. I don't want to talk about what happened, ok?" I just want to enjoy this . . . this one chance for it to be the three of us before reality slaps me back in the face. I focus on

Caden, relieved he's so little and has some time before life gets complicated. All he has to worry about right now is eating, sleeping, and pooping. Lucky.

Ryan looks like he's going to say something more so I brace myself. I'm terrified to hear whatever it is. He sighs deeply and runs his fingers through his hair. "We still have to figure some shit out, Brooks." He motions to Caden, and I know he's right. I thought I'd have more time to think of what to do . . . I don't even have any diapers at my apartment, let alone a crib or anything. Note to self: next time you break up with your baby daddy, pack a bigger bag.

Caden yawns and looks so content the tears automatically well up behind my eyes. So much for the chance to have his family together—I ruined it for my own scared, selfish reasons. *Well, kid, you're not even a day old and I've already screwed up your life. Best mom EVER.*

Ryan shifts closer, softening his voice as a single tear slips down my cheek and onto Caden's blanket. "Let me take you both home with me. At least for a couple of days?"

I squeeze my eyes shut and nod, snuggling Caden close to my chest.

I know being around Ryan with my confused feelings is a terrible idea, but I realize now how much I'm willing to sacrifice for my son. I'll do anything as long as it's what's best for him.

And who knows . . . maybe it will somehow magically be best for me, too.

CHAPTER

twenty-nine

One Week Old

Ryan

"DUDE, WHAT THE HELL ARE we feeding you?"

I look at Caden's innocent, unaware face and can't help but soften.

I also can't help but cringe as I see what a fucking bomb he left in his diaper.

The past week has been a crazy ride, learning everything there is to know about taking care of an entire person on the spot: He needs to eat like twelve times a day, doesn't like to sleep for more than two hours at a clip, and sometimes he even sleeps with his eyes open, which is pretty friggin' creepy.

We've been so busy taking care of Caden, trying to get some sleep ourselves, and entertaining visitors that Kelley and I have barely had a chance to see each other, let alone talk. When she's with Caden I try to work, and when I'm with him she tries to sleep. She was up with him most of the night, so right now I expect her to be out cold for a while. She mentioned in passing her mom was coming to stay with her to help with the baby, so I suppose that means she will be leaving soon. What did I expect— she'd come back here and everything would go back to normal? What the fuck is normal for us anyway?

I breathe through my mouth and try to keep from gagging as I change my son's offensive diaper. I get him cleaned up, making sure to cover his junk so he doesn't piss all over me (learned that one the hard way), and slide a new diaper on with an efficient, skilled execution. I feel like the fucking Pampers' Pit Crew. I go to pull the tabs on the diaper to secure it around his little body when I pull a little too hard and it rips. *Shit.* I reach for a new one stacked under the changing table to find it empty. *Double shit.*

Ok, I got this. Think, Blake, think. I look around the room and see my toolbox in the corner. *Bingo.* Holding Caden in place with one hand, careful he doesn't roll off the changing table, I reach for the toolbox with the other and feel around inside until my fingers grip what I'm searching for. I pull out a roll of duct tape and hold it up like it's the fucking Heisman Trophy before tearing off a piece big enough to wrap around Caden's lower half a few times. Once I secure the diaper in place, I lift him up to make sure it holds. Perfect.

"Your dad is a fucking genius, little man. I hope you get that from me." He wriggles his little legs and gurgles.

I lay him down in his crib, leaning over to study his face. I see so much of Kelley in him that it makes me smile. "But I hope you get a lot more from your mom. She's the fucking coolest and she's going to need you." I sadly shake my head. "I screwed up, and as much as I want to be there for both of you, I don't think your mom wants me around anymore. It's all my fucking fault, so don't ever think it's hers, ok? I'm going to need you to take care of her, though. Can you do that for me?" He blinks at me with his fierce blue eyes. Logically I'm aware he has no fucking clue what I'm talking about, but somehow it helps to say it out loud. "I'll hate myself for the rest of my fucking life knowing she doesn't believe I can be Mr. Right for her, so now it's up to you, kid. I know that's a lot of pressure to put on a guy, but she's worth it. I promise."

I rub my hand over his torso, trying to take a mental note of everything about him in this moment—how he looks, how he feels, how he smells. I know without a doubt he is the second best thing to ever happen in my life. The first is obviously seducing his mom at our best friends' wedding. She might be sorry about it, but I'm not. I don't regret it for one single second, and I never will.

Caden's face scrunches up as he yawns, and I know he's getting sleepy. I should probably let him fall asleep in his crib and try to grab a little shut-eye myself, but instead I scoop him up to cradle him in my arms. He gets restless, fighting sleep, so I rock him back and forth and try to soothe him by softly singing:

You are my sunshine, my only sunshine
You make me happy when skies are grey
You'll never know, dear, how much I love you
So please don't take my sunshine away

CHAPTER

thirty

Kelley

I WAKE UP FROM A dead sleep in a panic. It takes me a minute to adjust to my surroundings, and when I realize I'm in Ryan's bed I relax back into the pillows. I immediately sit back up, hating myself for forgetting this shouldn't be comfortable. I knew it would be hard to resist feeling all the same things I've always felt being here, but it's going to be even harder to leave a second time.

I slide out of bed to go check on Caden. As tired as I am you'd think sleep would come easy, but there is so much weighing on my heart and my mind he's the only thing that keeps me calm. Seeing him all small and content reminds me that nothing else matters and it was all worth it.

I shuffle down the hall to the nursery, silently in case he's sleeping. I freeze outside the door when I hear a voice. "Dude, what the hell are we feeding you?"

I smirk and press myself against the wall, peering into the room. Ryan's back is to me and I stifle a giggle as he grunts and makes gagging noises while cleaning Caden up. The diaper tab rips as he tries to secure it, and part of me thinks I should interrupt to let him know there are more in the closet. But a bigger part of me is curious to see what he does. When Ryan reaches for the toolbox and pulls out a roll of duct tape, I just about lose my shit laughing.

"Your dad is a fucking genius, little man. I hope you get that from me." I roll my eyes, but warmth blooms through my chest.

As Ryan puts Caden in his crib I know I should slip back to the bedroom and let them have their special father-son bonding moment, but my feet won't budge when I hear the next words that come out of Ryan's mouth.

"But I hope you get a lot more from your mom. She's the fucking coolest and she's going to need you. I screwed up, and as much as I want to be there for both of you, I don't think your mom wants me around anymore. It's all my fucking fault, so don't ever think it's hers, ok? I'm going to need you to take care of her, though. Can you do that for me?" There is a pause before Ryan adds, "I'll hate myself for the rest of my fucking life knowing she doesn't believe I can be Mr. Right for her, so now it's up to you, kid. I know that's a lot of pressure to put on a guy, but she's worth it. I promise."

I lean my head back against the wall, staring up at the ceiling, letting silent tears pour down my cheeks. It's all *my* fault for breaking this resilient, strong, honest man.

When I hear his soft, deep voice singing "You Are My Sunshine," I place my palm over my mouth, stifling a low, gut-wrenching sob as everything becomes painfully clear—Ryan Blake is what fate had in store for me all along.

m

A SHORT WHILE LATER I wait in the living room while Ryan finally gets Caden to sleep.

"Hey, you're up." He looks startled to see me as he walks into the room.

Not wanting to waste any time, or lose my nerve, I bite out, "Did you mean what you said?"

"What part?" he asks, confused.

"Everything you said at the beach, what you said after. All of it." I need to make sure one last time this isn't all in my head.

He stares at me, his jaw tense, not moving until finally he takes a step forward so we're mere inches apart. Without breaking our gaze he grinds out, "Every last fucking word."

Good enough for me. Without hesitation I launch myself forward at the exact moment he catches my face in his hands, our mouths meeting hard and fast. I moan into his mouth, needing him and his cinnamon taste as much as I need air. His fingers twist in my hair, bringing me so close I'm not sure where he ends and I begin.

Eventually he breaks away, resting his forehead on mine so we can each catch our breath. I hold onto his arms, refusing to allow him to let go of me. Not that he tries to.

He only pulls back slightly and grins at me in such a loving, irresistible, cocky way that the next thing I know I blurt out, "Will you marry me?"

Forget all the cliché fairy tales—this princess is finally going to fight for her prince for a change.

Rather than look surprised, Ryan looks pleasantly amused. "You know we're already married, right?"

"Well your proposals kind of sucked so it's my turn." We both chuckle before I get more serious. "I just want you to know that I'm choosing you, Blake. I love you and want to be with you, exactly as you are. I don't care what happened before and I don't care what might happen later on. I don't even care if you tell me you love me or not. As long as we both know we want this, right here, right now, that's all that matters."

Ryan grabs my chin with his thumb and forefinger, forcing me to look right into his sincere eyes. "I fucking love you, Brooks. Can't you see that? I'm *in* love with you. Madly, deeply, fucking stupid in love with you."

I smile, holding back my choked up emotions at finally hearing those words fall from his lips. That doesn't mean I still won't give him a hard time, though. "Shouldn't you be calling me 'Blake' now, too?" I tease.

"Trust me, nothing makes me prouder—or harder—to know you're mine . . . your body, your heart, and your name." He gives me a quick, but passionate, kiss on the lips, pressing his hard-on against my thigh to prove his point.

He pulls back with a cocky grin. "But you will always be Brooks to me, Sunshine."

I really wouldn't have it any other way.

Seven Weeks Old

Ryan

"WHAT THE FUCK? THEY'RE LATE. I'm going to kill your Uncle Lucas, Caden. Hope you're not too attached to the asshole."

"Hey!"

"Sorry. Hope you're not too attached to the butthole."

I pace back and forth from the living room to the kitchen, Caden resting on my shoulder.

Kelley laughs from the couch, making me growl. "It's not funny, Brooks."

Today is the first day Kelley and I are cleared to have sex since Caden was born, and Lucas and Kinsley were supposed to be here fifteen minutes ago to watch him for the night. I love the little guy, but tonight I need his mommy all to myself. I have a lot planned, and most of it involves her being naked with my dick inside her. Ok, pretty much all of it does.

Thank fucking god the door opens a second later and Kinsley and Lucas come barging in.

"So sorry we're late. We, um, lost track of time." Kinsley blushes while Luc doesn't look at all like he's sorry. From their rumpled hair and clothes, I can fucking guess what they were up to. The bastard actually looks smug. *Yeah, rub it in, you child-less prick. Just wait until a screaming kid causes you to have the worst case of blue balls imaginable.*

I practically toss Caden into Kinsley's arms—making sure to be gentle and giving him a quick kiss on the head—before grabbing Kelley's hand and our bag and dragging her to the door.

"What's the rush, Ry? You seem kind of on edge." Lucas leans back on the couch, stretching his arms and legs out. The jerk knows how long I've had to wait for tonight so he's being an ass on purpose.

I don't have time to sit here and argue with him, so I settle for shouting, "Screw you, Graham" as we leave the apartment.

Just before the door closes I hear him yell, "I thought you wanted to screw your wife?" I hear a soft thud that sounds like a hand smacking a shoulder. "What? I thought that's why we're babysitting tonight?"

Kelley laughs louder as I herd us into the elevator. Normally I'd find this shit funny as hell too, but right now I really just need a minute alone with my woman.

As soon as the elevator doors close I push her up against the side, silencing her laughter and eliciting a groan from the back of her throat. I thrust my tongue past her lips, savoring every dip and ripple of her mouth as I drink her in. I instinctively grind my hips against hers when I feel her do the same. God I've missed feeling her.

The elevator dings to indicate we're at the lobby so I reluctantly pull away. Kelley pouts in protest. I'm tempted to stay here and continue this all night too, but the surprise I have for her will be well worth the wait.

"ARE WE THERE YET?"

"No."

"How about now?"

Jesus, every fucking time with this girl. I grunt my frustration, but really I'd listen to her ask a million times.

As soon as I pass the sign that reads Peyton Cove, I can feel the excitement radiating off Kelley in waves.

The sun is just starting to set as I walk us out to the beach, to the same spot we promised forever. The beach is deserted, a big red blanket and picnic basket laid out before us, just as I requested. Let's just say Marge Brown has more pull in this town than I originally thought.

Kelley chokes up as she, too, remembers everything that happened here. I take her hands in mine, wanting her to know this time it will be different. Without saying a word, I reach into my pocket and pull out two rings—one a small, shiny diamond and the other a simple loop of twine.

After I slip them on her finger, I place a small kiss on top of them. "There. Back where they belong. Where they've always belonged."

I put my lips to hers, kissing her long and deep. I figure it's best not to get too caught up in words right now . . . they usually get us in trouble. I instead let my mouth, my hands, and my heart do the talking. They've always been better at expressing how I feel, anyway.

I guide Kelley down to lay on the blanket, coming to rest on top of her. I take a minute to stare at my beautiful fucking wife. Her long hair is down and flowing around her shoulders, her gorgeous eyes dancing with lust and love. She's wearing a white sundress, which really needs to go. I reach for the hem, pulling it up to reveal the fact she's wearing absolutely nothing underneath.

Man, I *really* fucking love her.

I shed my own clothes in record time and kiss my way across her skin. I trace my fingers up her thigh, gently roaming until I reach her softest flesh. I want to make sure she's ready for me, because once I start there will be no holding back with her. All or nothing from this point forward. For-fucking-ever.

I rub one finger over her clit until I hear her breath quicken, slowly pushing a finger inside to find her wet and willing. She grabs my ass to pull me closer, whimpering into my ear.

Not able to hold back any longer, I thrust inside her, fireworks exploding above us.

Literally . . . I hired a barge to set off fireworks as soon as the sun went down.

Kelley's eyes fly open in surprise. I grin like a damn cocky bastard and whisper warmly into her ear, "You always said you wanted fireworks, and I want to make sure you have everything you ever dreamed of."

The sparkle in her eyes is the most beautiful look I've seen on her yet, and trust me, she's *always* beautiful. She holds onto me tighter as we find our perfect pace, each giving and taking everything we need as sparks and color light up the sky around us.

The End.

Find out more

Want a little behind the scenes peek about the making of this book? Head on over to http://jshbooks.com/books/mad-addiction/behind-the-book/ for more!

acknowledgements

TO THE GREATEST HUSBAND EVER—CLIFFORD Peter, you are *my* sunshine.

To my family—Your excitement and support in this writing venture make me feel all sorts of warm and fuzzies.

To Kristine of Glass Paper Ink Bookblog and Erin Daniels of Read and Ramble Book Blog—Thank you for not only being such amazing fans of my first ever book, Crazy Beautiful, but for also being such sweet beta readers for this next one! To know Lucas, Kinsley, Kelley, and Ryan have such enthusiastic cheerleaders makes writing their stories even more fun.

To April Wells, Lydia at HEA Bookshelf, Maleesha at The Romance Room Blog, Megan Keith, Ang at PNR Book Lover Reviews, Tamara Roach, Jeananna at The Book Reading Gals, and the rest of you amazing bloggers—Words cannot describe how incredibly thankful I am you took the chance on a new author and said such lovely things <3

To Kari March—Thanks again for the beautiful cover design! (And putting up with my craziness! hah)

To Ellie at Love N. Books—I'm happy I found your name on that bathroom wall!

To Christine and Nichole at Perfectly Publishable—Thanks again for polishing this beauty up. Your attention to detail allows me to breathe a sigh of relief when it's time to send a book off into the world!

And finally, to anybody who takes a chance to read this— You have my heart. Thank you!

about the author

WHEN SHE'S NOT MAKING CONFETTI as head honcho over at The Confetti Bar (*theconfettibar.com*), co-dreaming with creative women through Monarch Workshop (*monarchworkshop.com*), and blogging about her health & wellness journey going sugar-free at Simple Unsweet (*simpleunsweet.com*), Jessica loves to spend her nights getting caught up in imaginary worlds.

She lives in central CT with her husband, Clifford, and the cutest cat EVER, named Curious.

She loves colorful things, making people smile, things that smell good, and is obsessed with lemon water. And glitter. Lots of glitter.

She also loves, well . . . love. (She's a sucker for a sweet story.)

You can check out what she's up to at *jshbooks.com* and on Instagram (@jshbooks)

Want to know anything else? Feel free to say hi at *lovejshbooks@gmail.com!*

www.ingramcontent.com/pod-product-compliance
Lightning Source LLC
Chambersburg PA
CBHW031728170626
46808CB00005B/1927

* 9 7 8 0 9 9 7 2 3 1 9 2 2 *